Lyons loo͟   ͟alley. It reeked ͟   ͟r.

"I'm telepathic, ͟   ͟I can see into the future. ͟

Carl Lyons laughed. "And what do you see for tonight?"

"Dead people, man. Dead people."

"Oh, yeah. Who?"

The Arab extended a greedy palm. "Five dollars, I tell your fortune. I tell you who dies."

"Why pay?" shrugged Lyons. "I'll find out soon enough...."

"Dick Stivers is brilliant.... Damn good stories, well structured, well paced, well written!"
—*Don Pendleton*

Mack Bolan's
ABLE TEAM

Mack Bolan's
PHOENIX FORCE

MACK BOLAN
The Executioner

Cairo Countdown

Dick Stivers

A GOLD EAGLE BOOK FROM

TORONTO · NEW YORK · LONDON

Dedicated to the eleven American agents whose reconnaissance flight was downed by the Russians in 1958. The men parachuted onto Soviet territory and were captured in the outskirts of Yerevan. The lost airmen have never been recovered by the United States.

First edition April 1983

ISBN 0-373-61205-2

Special thanks and acknowledgment to
Paul Hofrichter for his contributions to this work.

Printed in Canada

1

DUST BLURRED the parallel lines of lights. Engines whining, the unmarked, black-painted U-2A/B spy plane taxied onto the center runway of Cairo International. Inside the cockpit, the American pilot—wearing an oxygen suit stripped of all insignia and marks of manufacture—spoke into his microphone, "This is Executive Underwriters' shuttle jet requesting permission for takeoff...."

"Permission granted," an accented voice told him. "Crosswinds of five kilometers per hour. Visibility three kilometers."

"No problem. On my way up."

The engine noise rose to a shriek, and the spy plane rolled forward, gathering speed. The Pratt & Whitney J75-P-13 engine generated 17,000 pounds of thrust, pressing the pilot back against his form-fitted seat. In seconds, the landing-gear wheels left the smooth asphalt of the runway. The hundred-foot-wide wings flexed in the slight crosswind.

Gaining altitude, the pilot banked to the east. The flight would take him first over the Gulf of Suez, the Sinai, Saudi Arabia, then Iraq to the Shatt al-Arab, where the armies of Iraq and Iran fought their vicious war of attrition. The high-altitude photos and electronic surveillance would allow the intelligence agencies of the United States to assess the casualties and destruction of the latest battle between the Iranian fanatics and the Iraqi defenders.

Below the spy plane, the lights of Cairo spread across the desert. The pilot watched his radar screens for any possible commercial flights crossing his flight path. Three blips appeared simultaneously, shooting upward from the slums circling the metropolitan center.

"This is Executive Underwriters' shuttle to Executive Center—"

Even as the pilot spoke, he died, a Soviet-made SAM-7 heat-seeking antiaircraft missile exploding in the exhaust vent of his engine.

Flaming debris that had been an American pilot and a top-secret multimillion-dollar aircraft fell to the Egyptian desert.

"WE HAD A UNIT WATCHING the place when they sent up the rocket," Bob Hershey told the agents assembling in the living room of a luxury home in the Cairo suburban quarter of Heliopolis. Hershey, a middle-aged CIA officer, had the look of a college athlete gone gray. He wore slacks and an undershirt. He spoke to the agents as he slipped on a tailored Kevlar vest and pressed the Velcro closures.

"It's an old apartment house," he continued. "We've got the place circled."

"We're going to take them?" an unshaven agent asked.

"Damn right. I sent Hopper and McGraw out there—they were the only other guys on duty. Told them to tail any of the crazies who leave. We're waiting for our liaison team now."

"You call all the discos?" an agent joked as he checked thirty-round Uzi mags.

"Didn't need to, Parks. I gave Sadek a pager. Got sick of calling nightclubs and apartments and whorehouses. Now we got direct communications with our playboy prince...."

The men laughed despite the tension. Then headlights swept the draperies as tires screeched around the circular driveway. Car doors opened, slammed closed.

"Speak of the devil..." Hershey said.

The four CIA men turned as Salah Abul Sadek burst through the room's double doors. A ranking officer of the Egyptian secret police and liaison to the CIA soldiers operating in Cairo, Sadek wore a lavender disco suit with a matching wide-brimmed hat. One of his men, in a wrinkled gray suit, followed him, a folding-stock Kalashnikov slung casually over a shoulder.

"Yet another attack?" Sadek asked in his British-accented English. "It was that airplane, am I correct?"

"One of our jets as it left the airport," Hershey told him.

"The bastards! Will it never stop? Does your embassy have a statement for the newspapers?"

"That's the ambassador's worry." Hershey slipped on his suit jacket, tucked Uzi mags in the coat's wallet pockets. "What we're going to do is stop those fanatics. Tonight."

WIND BANGED A COCA-COLA SIGN. Dust swirled on the street's stones, the wind from the desert carrying litter and the stink of the slums. Three Fiats followed an alley-narrow street through a district of shops and tenements. Yellow light spilled from the windows. One neon sign, Arabic symbols in electric blue, marked a shop.

In the lead car, Hershey spoke into his hand radio. "Park here."

Holding his Uzi under his suit coat, he left the car. He gingerly stepped through the piles of garbage and broken glass in the gutter, stopped at the end of the street. Parks and Sadek left their cars to join him. Hershey looked around the corner, pointed. "There."

Only stones and twisted metal remained of the first structure on the street. The second building, a shop with a second floor of rooms, leaned visibly, ready to fall. Beams scavenged from the wreckage of the collapsed building braced the leaning wall. Light showed in a corrugated sheet-metal hut on the roof of the tenement. Hershey pointed to a battered truck parked on a sidewalk.

"There's our surveillance. Hopper and McGraw are down on the other end. Those crazies with the rocket launcher are still in there."

"What about the people around here?" Parks indicated the dark shops and windows of the streets. "We go in and someone opens up shooting, and we're in an international incident."

Hershey sneered at his aide. "Maybe you want to call the police? They killed an American pilot tonight. We're going in there hard and fast. Sadek, any of the city police show up, show them your identification, keep them back. I want to take prisoners. Maybe we can break this group tonight."

"Certainly." The Egyptian slapped dust from his lavender nightclub finery.

"Hopper, McGraw," Hershey said into his hand radio. "Four of us are going in. You ready?"

"Yes, sir," an agent answered.

"Everyone else stay in your cars, keep the engines running. Acknowledge."

Several voices answered. Hershey turned to Parks. "Load and lock. I'm going first."

"Sir, I don't like this. We're exceeding our authority in a very questionable situation. Anything could—"

"I don't give a damn what you think!" Hershey raged. He keyed his hand radio. "Hopper, McGraw, go for the door." He turned to his aide. "You're transferring back to Langley, Parks. I won't have losers on my staff. But tonight you're following me."

Not waiting for Parks, Hershey left the shadows. He strode across the wide street paved with stone and patches of asphalt. Fifty yards away, two other Americans in conservative gray suits walked through the light of a street lamp, their right hands under their coats to conceal Uzis.

Parks snapped back the cocking handle of his Uzi, checked the thumb safety. He turned to the Egyptian liaison officer. "Wish us luck, Sadek."

"*Inshallah*, American."

One step into the street, Parks saw blood spray from the back of his superior. Hershey flew back, high-velocity AK slugs ripping him. Parks threw himself to the stones as slugs cracked past him. He rolled, scrambled back as autorifles fired burst after burst.

A rocket shrieked from one of the tenement's windows. The surveillance truck exploded in a flash of flame. Backed into the cover of a doorway, Parks saw Hershey struggling to raise himself from the pavement. Down the street, McGraw tried to drag Hopper to shelter. Another rocket streaked from the tenement. The two CIA soldiers disappeared in the blast, only rags and shredded flesh remaining of their bodies.

The lavender of his disco suit glowing in the light of the flames and street lamps, Sadek sprinted into the street, the pistol in his hand popping shots at the riflemen. Parks watched AK slugs spark off the stones as the Egyptian grabbed for Hershey. Then Parks lifted his Uzi, fired burst after burst through the windows of the building across the street. He aimed at the shadow of the man with a rocket launcher. He held down the trigger. Nine-millimeter slugs from his Uzi pocked the old walls, shattered glass.

Sadek grabbed Hershey's arms and dragged him over the pavement. Parks tore another thirty-round magazine from his coat pocket. He jammed it in his Uzi. Firing wild, he sent bursts through windows and into the sheet metal of the tenement's rooftop shanties.

Another terrorist with a rocket launcher appeared on the roof. The terrorist leaned over the wall and pointed the RPG at Sadek and Hershey. Parks fired without sighting his weapon. Slugs chipped the stone, hammered the corrugated shack behind the terrorist as he ducked back, the rocket flashing across the road to slam into a building.

Stones showered the men. A rolling cloud of dust

enveloped the street. Parks saw his one chance to survive, took it, sprinted through the cloud. The ancient dust was acrid in his fear-dry throat.

Dodging around the corner, he fell over Hershey and Sadek. The Egyptian was fumbling at the officer's wounds. The agents who had stayed in the cars—the two CIA men and the Egyptian with the folding AK—dragged Hershey into the cover of a shop entry, ripped open their superior's jacket. One man tore open a packet of field dressings. Parks looked at Hershey, saw an entry hole above his left eye, then saw the vast hole in the back of his head.

"Forget it, he's gone. Bring up the cars, we've got to get out of here." He keyed his hand radio. "Any of you that are still alive, report. Report."

No one answered.

SHOUTING PRAISES OF ALLAH, the voices of his warriors shook the concrete of the warehouse. The Libyan technician turned up the volume of the tape recorder. He listened to the instructions of the American officer, then the shooting and screaming, the rocket explosions, the fear and panic as the infidels died.

"Any of you that are still alive, report. Report."

Only silence answered the American.

Omar laughed. "That is all?"

"Then they communicate by encoded radio. With the other spies in their embassy, I think. I will have the courier take the tape to Damascus."

"Good, good." Omar left the electronics room, strode down the corridor of offices to the cavernous central area of the warehouse. He paused before stepping farther.

Looking at himself in the glass of an office window, he straightened his tie, the button-down collar of his shirt. He brushed lint from the gray wool Italian-tailored suit his role forced him to wear. He hated the clothing of the foreigners. Yet his assignment required a "modern" appearance. His daily routine as international banker and part-time diplomat to the Europeans required the imported tailored suit and shirts, the gold rings on his fingers, the American watch on his wrist, the Mercedes sedan. All served to delude the degenerates of Cairo, foreign and Egyptian.

He brushed back his hair, smoothed his eyebrows. Glancing sideways at his sharp profile, he imagined his face on the televisions of the world.

If Allah wills.... No! If Omar el-Riadh wills! Allah acts through his warriors. The will of Omar and Allah shall be one in conquest and empire.

With a final glance at the immaculate grooming of his reflection, Omar stepped out onto stairs. He stood looking down for a moment on his warriors assembled in the warehouse.

His warriors. Arabs and Africans. True followers of Allah from Egypt, Jordan, Syria and Libya. Front-line Palestinians who had tired of their leaders' empty promises. Volunteers from Chad and Angola.

Some of the men now tended to the reloading of the trucks carrying the Soviet SAM-7 missiles. Concealed in the interior of trucks, the missiles could be fired by the driver or by remote radio command. Other men, the warriors who had killed the Americans, cleaned their weapons, talking loudly and laughing while their comrades crowded around. Like himself, his warriors wore costumes: the rags of the fellaheen, the polyester of the urban poor, the foreign styles of the bourgeoisie.

They saw him, turned as one to their leader. Voices shouted out praises of Allah, Mustafa, Omar and Khaddafi. His men flourished their rocket launchers and AK-47 rifles. Omar raised his arms. The voices faded to rapt silence.

"Warriors! Praise Allah!" he called.

He had to wait for the shouts to fade again.

"Tonight Allah gave us victory over the cursed foreigners, the infidels, the American dogs of Zion. It is only one victory of many. Their spy jets shall fall in flames, the dog mercenaries of Israel and Satan shall fall beneath the swords of Allah, their cities shall be reduced to dust.

"You, the warriors of the one glorious Creator shall be above all others, you shall be honored by all peoples. You shall be princes over the people.

"You, the front-line warriors of the holy jihad shall walk on the rotting flesh of the Israelis and the Americans; you shall erect the Mosque of Victory on a mountain of bones; the world shall be your empire."

Omar el-Riadh raised his arms to the steel and concrete of the ceiling of the warehouse. "The prophet foretold of our victory. Allah himself guides our swords."

The words came in one roar from all the assembled terrorists, *"Allah Akbar!"*

2

RACKS OF WEAPONS covered one wall of Andrzej
Konzaki's laboratory. Oak workbenches at wheelchair height lined two other walls. Heavy machines
spaced throughout the floor area—a lathe, a drill
press, an hydraulic press, a band saw, grinders and
buffers—gave the large room the look of a factory.
Windows viewing the farmlands and mountains
around Stony Man dominated the fourth wall.

While Konzaki put the tiny wheel of a Foredom
polisher to the chamber of a modified Atchisson assault shotgun, Carl Lyons surveyed the collection of
weapons. He took an MP-40 "Schmeisser" from the
rack. Swinging out the wire stock of the World War II
submachine gun, he put it to his shoulder, sighted
through the window to a distant mountainside. Returning the weapon to the rack, he scanned the other
rifles and submachine guns and heavy automatic
weapons—American, British, French, German,
Soviet, ComBloc. Obsolete and modern, the weapons
represented the recent history of the world, war after
war after war consuming the resources and technolog-
ical genius of nations, wasting their wealth, maiming
and murdering their young men. Devices of tragedy.

But marvelous and fascinating. He took a 1903
30-06 Springfield from the rack, snapped back the

bolt to check the magazine and chamber. The weapon's steel shone with oil. In World War I, a soldier had won the Congressional Medal of Honor with the later model of the 30-06, the P-16 Enfield. His deadly, unrelenting rifle fire had convinced a company of German troops that they faced an overwhelming enemy force. And they had. One American with a rifle. That one soldier, Sergeant York, accepted the surrender of one hundred thirty-two Germans and marched them to the rear.

"A thousand-yard killer," Konzaki called out. "Put a nine-power scope on that and you could hit a target on the horizon."

"No doubt about it." Lyons returned the old rifle to its place.

"And I'm working on over-the-horizon capability," Konzaki joked. "Come look at this Atchisson. It's ready to test."

The black metal-and-plastic assault weapon looked like an oversize M-16 but fired 12-gauge shotshells semiauto, three-round bursts, or full-auto bursts. A box magazine held seven standard or Magnum rounds. Lyons had used an Atchisson in the Amazon, when Able Team and their Xavante allies fought Khmer Rouge slave-raiders. In three vicious, no-quarter firefights, in the rain forest, on a moonlit river, in a warlord's fortress, the Atchisson meant the difference between victory or death.*

"This one has a fourteen-inch barrel and a telescoping stock." Konzaki pressed a lever and pulled out the tubing of the buffer-spring/stock assembly to full length.

*Able Team #4, *Amazon Slaughter*.

Lyons took the Atchisson, tried the weight and balance. "Like a CAR-15." He jerked the padded buttplate against his shoulder, tried a snap-aim on the band saw. Then he pressed the release lever, slid in the stock and held the gun at waist height, assault style.

"Lighter than the other one," he commented.

"Less barrel, less plastic and steel, more titanium," Konzaki said. "The rate of fire and the shot patterns created by the short barrel give the weapon an awesome potential value in an urban firefight. After I read through the debriefing reports of the Amazon action, I went ahead with this SWAT version."

"What that Atchisson did to people and things.... You just would not believe it."

"Yes, I would," Konzaki replied, his words sober, without enthusiasm or humor, simply stating a fact. "And I also went back to work on the Berettas."

Konzaki palmed his wheelchair's thin tires in opposite directions, spinning the chair about. Rubber squeaked on the concrete as he propelled himself the length of the workbench. He skidded to a stop at a cabinet.

For a moment, Lyons hesitated. In the long last morning of horror in the slave-city of the Chinese plutonium lord, Lyons had cursed the Beretta. The silent 9mm autopistol required perfect head shots for an instant kill. Underpowered to avoid the crack of the bullets breaking the speed of sound, the slugs had failed to knock down the enraged, adrenaline charged men that Lyons had faced. As if trapped within a nightmare, he had shot men again and again, spraying bursts of lightweight subsonic slugs into their chests and faces only to see the men continue toward him. It had been the fifteen-round magazine of a Beretta 93-R that had saved Lyons from death.

The weapon represented long hours of meticulous, frustrating work for Konzaki. How could Lyons politely refuse the weaponsmith's latest modification?

Never mind the polite words. He could talk straight with the ex-marine. Konzaki knew more than Lyons about combat.

"Forget it, Andrzej. No more Berettas. Not for me. They're great for special occasions, but my personal experience tells me that when the going gets rough, the Berettas aren't enough."

"So I put together a hybrid—"

"Forget it!" Lyons snapped. "No diamond points, no steel cores, no high-tech modifications. I've had it with 9mm. From now on, I'm carrying a silenced MAC-10."

"How about a .45-caliber ACP? Suppressed Colt Government Model? Semiauto and three-shot burst? Full-powered loads? Subsonic but full powered? Want to see it?"

Lyons laughed. "Yeah. Sure do."

Hard rubber squeaked on the concrete. Konzaki wheeled back to Lyons with a plastic tray on his lap. "There's one and only one policy in this workshop: Mack Bolan and his soldiers get the weapons they want. They get research and quality, but first they get what they want. Here it is."

He lifted away the tray's lid. Lyons saw a

Parkerized-black Colt automatic fitted with a blunt suppressor. He took the weapon from its bed of silicon cloth, pressed the release to drop the empty magazine, slipped back the slide, locked it.

The slide had been modified and shortened, the barrel machined to accept the oval cylinder of the suppressor. A fold-down lever and enlarged trigger guard provided a two-handed hold. The arc of the safety continued into the grip, became a fire selector. Like the markings on the Beretta, a single white dot and three dots indicated semiauto and three-shot full-auto bursts.

"You're a genius."

"And you only see the obvious changes," Konzaki responded. "I've worked on that off and on since I received the Berettas. Basically, I pirated the Beretta design. I had to machine a new slide, a custom-locking block assembly, a new barrel, sear mechanism. I increased the twist of the barrel's rifling to cut the bullet velocity and increase the accuracy. The suppressor started out at over a foot in length. Look at it now—the entire pistol length comes to only twelve inches. Somewhat awkward compared to the standard Army-issue pistol, but considering...."

"This is fantastic. And it fires full-powered rounds?"

"Most .45 cartridges don't go supersonic. Hot loads, maybe. But your standard ball rounds, with the increased twist of the barrel, no. This weapon will throw a 230-grain slug at a thousand feet per second to generate over four hundred pounds of muzzle energy. Hollowpoints deliver almost as much energy and more shock power. The subsonic nines never produced more than two hundred.''

"Where's the ammo? Let's go shooting!''

"Look at the magazines. The pistol accepts not only the standard seven-round magazine, but extended ten- and fifteen-round magazines. Someone does manufacture a thirty-round magazine but it's almost two feet long.''

"Tell me more!''

Konzaki laughed. "Like a kid with a new toy.''

BUMPING OVER A BACK COUNTRY ROAD, Konzaki swerved the hand-controlled pickup around rocks and ruts. Lyons loaded an Atchisson drum magazine with twenty rounds of double-ought number-two steel buckshot. On the seat between the men, a clutter of magazines, weapons and aluminum canes rattled with every bump.

The Virginia hills glowed in the morning light, spring leaves brilliant against smears of raw earth and vividly green grass. The truck splashed through mud and rainwater, swerved through a space in the fence.

"Where we going?'' Lyons asked, jamming the last round in the drum magazine.

"Don't know. Just wandering around.''

"Don't go anywhere with people. Or county sheriffs. Who needs trying to explain this Atchisson. . . .''

Konzaki left the tire-rutted pasture, wove through trees. An eroded hillside appeared. The legless man jerked back the brake bar, put the automatic transmission in neutral.

"Look like a backstop to you?'' he asked Lyons, pointing to the sheer dirt wall of the hill.

"Good enough."

Konzaki grabbed his canes, swung out of the truck. The spring clamps were tight around his huge forearms as his fists gripped the handles. He moved fast, using artificial legs and the canes to steady himself on the matted woodland debris. He took ear protectors from the open back of the pickup, tossed a set to Lyons, jammed a pair on his own head. Then he lifted out a folding table and a folding chair.

"Need any help with those things?" Lyons asked.

"No problem. It's all modified." A strap on the table went over one shoulder, a strap on the chair over the other. "I do this all the time. By myself, with my kids. With Julie. My wife works in an office in State. Never gets any exercise. We go out in the country, I have to carry all the things. She can't walk a mile on broken ground without blisters."

"Bet you never get blisters," bantered Lyons. "Even with new shoes."

He followed Konzaki across the road. A cleared section of woods allowed a firing lane. Stumps here and there jutted out of the grass and ferns. A smiling Konzaki found a place without mud, set down the table, unfolded the legs, put the table on its feet.

"There's another chair in the truck. And get the milk crate and the sandbag."

In a few minutes, they had chairs and a shooting table assembled. A fresh breeze swayed the trees around them. Konzaki leaned back in his chair, stared up at the branches and the blue sky.

"This is great!" he shouted out, his breath still clouding slightly in the early spring air. He turned to

Lyons. "The Agency was strictly suit and tie, all day long, every day. Never again."

"Hey, man. I didn't come out here to picnic...."

"So shoot something! You waiting for permission? Put that twenty-round magazine on the Atchisson, see if you can burn it out."

"Is that a dare?" Lyons grinned. He lifted the gun from the crate and jammed the drum magazine in the assault shotgun as he stood up. He snapped the stock to his shoulder and fired.

High-velocity steel balls blasted tree stumps as Lyons whipped the sights from one target to another, firing semiauto single shots.

"Three-round bursts!" Konzaki shouted.

Flicking down the fire selector one click, Lyons sighted on a tree fifty feet away, fired again. The weapon slammed his shoulder back, but he held the sights in line. A storm of steel shredded the side of the tree, ripped leaves and branches from the brush behind it.

"Again!"

Another tree went to pieces, then another.

"Full auto! Empty it!"

Lyons pushed the lever down all the way, dropped the weapon to his waist, walked forward, pulled back the trigger. Straining against the recoil, he continued forward, spraying several trees with a maelstrom of high-velocity steel. Branches exploded in bursts of chopped debris, wood flew, bark showered the ground. Finally the Atchisson's action locked back.

"Now put in another magazine, load the first round, but don't fire!"

"Yeah, sure." Lyons felt queasy from the recoil

beating; his hands were numb, his teeth ached. He dropped the empty drum, pushed in a seven-round box mag and burned his hand on the receiver when he hit the action release to strip off the first shotshell.

"Damn, it's hot."

"Hold it away from you. It might pop...."

They waited a few seconds, then Konzaki took the Atchisson from Lyons and released the magazine. He turned the ejection port to the ground, snapped back the actuator. When the shotshell hit the dirt, he shifted his left leg to set his foot down on top of the hot shell.

"What're you doing?"

"If it explodes from the chamber heat, I can buy a new foot...."

Hinging open the weapon, Konzaki looked into the receiver. "Ever notice that shotgun shells aren't brass?"

"Nah, man. Thought brass came in designer colors."

"Look. Melted plastic in the chamber. This shell—" Konzaki stooped down, picked up the cooled round "—would have been fused in there. No full-auto firefights with the Atchisson until I come up with improved casings."

Lyons laughed. "Andy, firefights with the Atchisson don't last that long."

"Maybe aluminum."

"Now the .45."

Slapping in a magazine, he pulled back the slide of the autopistol to feed a round. He held the piece with both hands—right hand on the grip, left hand on the fold-down lever, left thumb hooked through the oversize trigger guard. He sighted over the phosphorous sights at a distant tree and squeezed off a shot.

He heard the slug smash into the wood. But no muzzle blast. He slipped off his ear protectors, fired again. The crack of the slug punching into the tree broke the woodland silence. He aimed into the air, fired, finally heard the muzzle sound: not a blast, more a rushing sound. Sudden, then over. The slug zipped off into empty sky.

Lyons set the safety as he turned to Konzaki. "This is it! When will it be ready?"

"When do you need it?"

A shrill beep came from the pocket of Lyons's jacket. The tone repeated three times. Then three times again. Both men knew what the code meant.

"Now."

3

IN THE TOURIST SECTION of the crowded airliner, Blancanales studied sales brochures and notebooks of technical information. He reviewed the prices, uses and specifications of the agricultural plumbing of his imaginary company. Three rows in front of him, Carl Lyons also read from notebooks. The tourists around them slept, or chatted or practiced their Arabic phrases.

Ten hours of flying numbed his mind. But he ignored the voices and laughter around him, concentrated on the photos of plastic plumbing fittings. Rows of numbers and prices went double. He looked out his window to the patchwork of fields and farms and irrigation canals below him. He looked beyond the fertile Nile Delta to the distant windswept desert spanning the horizon, resting his eyes for a moment on the desolation. Then he returned to his study. Only a few minutes remained until they landed at Cairo International Airport. His life, and the lives of Lyons and Gadgets, might depend on his knowledge of the products and the company that he supposedly represented.

This mission had Blancanales concerned. Unlike the other times Mack Bolan had sent them into action, they had no knowledge of what to expect. Hal

Brognola, on the Air Force flight across the Atlantic, had told them only that they would work in Cairo with Yakov Katzenelenbogen, the one-armed ex-officer of the Israeli Mossad, now leader of Bolan's Phoenix Force. No briefings, no maps, no photos, no information on their opponents. Because they would take commercial flights from London to Egypt, then pass through Egyptian customs, they did not carry weapons. Just phony identification as businessmen and notebooks of sales material from their "companies."

An electronic chime rang. Blancanales looked up to see a sign flashing Fasten Seat Belts/No Smoking in English, French and Arabic.

"Ladies and gentlemen," a proper British voice announced, "we will soon begin our descent to Cairo International Airport. Please fasten your safety belts and remain seated until the...."

The voice droned on, repeating the announcement in other languages as the flight attendants went up and down the aisle, checking seat belts, adjusting seats, gathering soft-drink containers and tumblers.

Below them, the green of the delta became sprawling suburbs, modern city, slums: narrow streets and wide highways. Blancanales closed his notebook only when the jet lost altitude, dropping flaps for the landing descent.

Here I go, Blancanales thought. *Where and what for, I hope someone knows.*

GADGETS SCHWARZ closed the door behind the bell-boy and surveyed the plush room. Despite the Egyptian decor and the window that looked out over

Cairo, he stood in plastic fantastic America. The room smelled of antiseptic and air freshener. The air-conditioning unit whirred faintly. A tourist guide to the city lay by the phone. The maids had stretched the bed cover tight, polished the furniture and television, left tiny bars of scented soap for him. He went to the television, switched it on. Kojak shouted in Arabic, grabbed a long-legged blonde.

"Wow," Gadgets laughed. "First class. . . ."

The phone rang. Startled, he stared at it a second, letting it ring again, then took it.

"Your assistant is here, sir," a clerk intoned in perfect English. "Would it be convenient for you to receive him in your room?"

"Yeah, sure. Send him up."

"Certainly, sir."

Schwarz turned the television up loud, went to the mosaic-tile-and-blue-enamel bathroom. The tiles were decorated with hieroglyphs and stylized scenes. Splashing water on his face, he rinsed away the dust, tried a packet of the hotel's scented hand lotion as tires shrieked, bullets ricocheted in the next room. Then his assistant knocked.

A young Egyptian stood in the corridor with two aluminum cases. "Well, hey, man," the Egyptian drawled in Tex-Mex. He extended his hand. "Here I am. I'm. . . ."

Without a word, Gadgets motioned him inside. The young man grunted with the weight of the cases, staggered across the room to the bed, put the cases down. Gadgets snapped the first one open.

A fiberboard packing box filled half the interior. Stenciled words spelled out the manufacturer:

European Defence Products. To identify the product, someone had lettered with marking pen, "2 Armbursts." Gadgets was pleased. Unlike the shoulder-launched RPG-7 and LAAW rockets, this German-manufactured weapon produced no deadly backblast. A charge inside the disposable tubes propelled the rocket and a counter-mass in opposite directions. The counter-mass, a kilogram of harmless plastic chips, sprayed behind the launcher as the rocket shot from the tube. The rocket's propellant then accelerated the warhead to a speed of six feet per second. And Able Team now had two of them!

In the other half of the case, a battlejacket of Kevlar and steel wrapped an Uzi and a bundle of magazines. Gadgets saw a second weapon, a silenced Beretta 93-R, with custom shoulder holster and several magazines of subsonic rounds.

Gadgets snapped open the second case. He found radios, electronic units, ammunition. Taking out one small device, he switched on the power and pulled out an antenna. He turned in a circle slowly, waving the antenna at the walls of the hotel room. He touched the antenna to the telephone, walked into the bath, then returned to the Egyptian and waved the unit over him.

"I got no electric cooties!" the guy said.

"Supercool," Gadgets commented. He took a hand radio from the case, keyed the transmit. "Man Number Three speaking.... Who's out there?"

"I am," Carl Lyons answered.

"You swept your room yet?"

"This is your International Fluid Technology sales

representative,'' proclaimed the voice of Rosario Blancanales.

"Both of you," Gadgets interrupted, "don't talk until you've checked your rooms. In fact, forget it. I'm in 505. Meet me here. Have your assistants watch the equipment."

"You one paranoid hombre," the Egyptian told him.

"You got a name?"

"Mohammed. You can call me Mo. I'm talking the Arab talk for you, driving your car, showing you the sights. Mr. One-Hand told me this might be a real party, wild times. He said you guys are hardcore cowboys."

"Who do you work for?"

Mohammed grinned. "You! Ask me another tough one."

"Your name Mo as in Mossad?"

"Who's that dude?"

"Okay, that's cool. You look Egyptian. I guess you speak the language like one?"

"I am one, man. I talk it mucho perfecto. Want to hear?"

"Hope you speak it better than you do English...."

Mohammed shammed offense. "Hey, wait a minute—"

Knuckles tapped the door. "Later. Right now, take a walk."

The jiving Mohammed gave Blancanales and Lyons a quick salute as he left. Lyons squinted an eye at the young man, then closed the door and locked it.

"Konzaki include those Armburst rockets in your CARE package?" Blancanales asked.

"Sure did. Rockets, Uzi, Kevlar battlesuit with trauma plates. I think we're into something heavy here—"

"How do we verify those three kids?" Lyons interrupted.

"My man had the right ID," Gadgets answered.

"What identification?"

"There...." He pointed to the equipment in the aluminum cases.

"Not good enough."

"We'll talk to Katz," Blancanales told them. "I want to know exactly what goes on. Immediately."

"Conference call." Gadgets pulled another radio from the case, selected a frequency. "The Wizard calling," he said into the mouthpiece. "Team waiting. Wizard calling...." Repeating his code, Gadgets checked his watch.

"This is Phoenix One," Yakov Katzenelenbogen answered in his upper-class English soldier's accent. "I trust you had a pleasant flight."

Lyons leaned to the radio to cut off the pleasantries. "Request positive identification of assistants. Absolute positive."

"I watched the young men enter the hotel. I assure you of their identity and trustworthiness."

Blancanales squatted beside the bed and reached for the radio. Gadgets pointed to the handset in his pocket. "Use your own. Your signal will be relayed to Katz."

Keying his hand radio, Blancanales asked: "Is there surveillance? Can we meet for a conference?"

"No! Coded radio only. We cannot risk a meeting. Allow me to explain...." He briefed them on the destruction of the secret U-2, then the ambush of the CIA squad. As he detailed his investigation of the incidents, the three men of Able Team looked to one another.

When the ex-Mossad agent—the unofficial leader of Phoenix Force—voiced his conclusion, the words came as no surprise. "I believe the Muslim Brotherhood has penetrated the Central Intelligence Agency."

4

IN A TAXI moving through the traffic of Sharia el-Corniche, Lyons monitored Katz speaking with an Egyptian in Arabic, the conversation meaningless to the ex-LAPD cop. Limousines and little Fiats, crowded buses with young men riding on the bumpers and hanging from the windows passed the slow-moving taxi. On the curb, tourists leaving hotels waved for the taxi. Abdul the driver waved back, indicating Lyons in the back seat. To the west, the late afternoon sun flashed from the Nile.

"You three Yanks are lucky," Abdul told Lyons. "This is the tourist season. If Colonel Katzenelenbogen didn't have the friends he does in Cairo, this operation would be much more difficult for you. Hotel rooms, rental cars, trustworthy translators...."

"Yeah, helps to be tight with the Mossad, right?"

"Sir! As I told you before—"

"Cut the crap. You're Israeli. Who else could say Katzen...Katzenelen...Katzenelenbogenlogen! I mean, I work with Katz, and I can't even say his name."

"I speak several languages. It is a gift from Allah."

"Yeah, yeah. Let's just keep it straight. You know

who I work for, and I know who you work for. I don't mind an allied effort here.''

"I can only repeat, sir, that I am an Egyptian.''

"Like I said, allies.'' Lyons ignored him, keyed his hand radio. "Wizard. Politician. We're turning off the Nile Boulevard. We're passing...." He leaned forward to Abdul. "What's the name of that hotel there?''

"Shepheard's. We're leaving the Corniche, turning east at the Sharia el-Hamy...."

"We'll be at the embassy in less than a minute. You got them in sight?''

Gadgets answered. "Jam time. Some bus lost a wheel. The cars with Katz and the station officer and Sadek are still on the embassy grounds. Pass up this street and go on to the next boulevard, circle back. You catching Katz's conversation clear?''

"Sure, loud and clear, hearing every word. But don't understand nothin'. What's the point of—''

"Be cool, man. If Katz wants us to hear something, he'll say it in English. That Parks guy—the assistant to the dear departed station chief—his Arabic is way bad, so we'll hear English again when he gets back in Katz's limo.''

Blancanales's voice came on. "Ironman, you're impatient. Just relax, tough guy. Play tourist. People pay money to come here. Could be mucho worse.''

"Like how? We don't know the language. We don't know the city. We don't know who we're after. All we can do is follow Katz and a crew of CIA screw-ups and wait for those ragheads to hit them....''

"Like I say,'' said Blancanales. "Could be much worse....''

"Like how?" Lyons demanded.

"You want to cruise around in that limo?" Gadgets asked. "Cruise around waiting for an RPG to come through the window?"

"Ah...yeah, you got a point. We're turning on the boulevard. Hey, Abdul, what's the name of this street?" Lyons asked.

"Sharia el-Qasr el-Aini."

"Yeah, the main drag. What did they just say in the limo?"

"Parks is back," Gadgets answered. "They're on their way to the airport."

"Ironman," Blancanales's voice came over the hand radio again. "Keep your distance. Tell your driver to start for the airport."

"Will do. Over."

Behind an old bus, Gadgets watched diesel smoke swirl around the taxi. The bus driver and several passengers crowded around the rear of the stricken vehicle. Two men rolled a wheel through the bumper-to-bumper traffic, weaving between cars, imploring drivers to back up, motioning other drivers to halt. But it was purposeless. The rear axle of the bus had snapped. In front of Schwarz's taxi, the bus driver argued with the passengers, waving his arms, motioning for them to leave the bus. Drivers trapped in traffic screamed at the bus driver and the drivers around them. Horns sounded in an unending cacophony.

"I tell you," Mohammed said in the front seat, "these people, they loco. The bus, it breaks down. They think a horn will make it go. These streets, they crazy place."

"You learn to talk like that on a kibbutz?"

"Oh, yeah, man. Kibbutzy on the Rio Grande."

Gadgets's hand radio buzzed. "Politician here. Cars coming out of the embassy."

"We can't go anywhere."

"We can. Break free when you get the chance."

On the other side of the Sharia Latin America, Cairo police stepped into traffic, blew whistles, held up white-gloved hands. The gates of the American Embassy opened. The tan-uniformed cops held traffic back as a Fiat with Cairo police department markings led two black Lincoln Continental limousines from the compound. The three cars accelerated away and swept around a corner.

Two teenagers on motor scooters darted past the officers holding traffic. One policeman blew a whistle at them. The other officer called to his partner. They hurried to return from the street to their positions at the gate. With clouds of exhaust clouding around the cars, the wall of traffic rushed forward.

As Blancanales passed in his taxi, Gadgets keyed his hand radio. "You see those two on motorbikes?"

"Looked like students."

"Big rush to get to school, too much of a rush."

"I'll watch for them."

"We'll get out of this jam as soon as we can. Later."

Weaving through the traffic, the driver of Blancanales's taxi, a taciturn, methodical young man named Zaki, kept one foot on the accelerator, the other on the brake, speeding to close the distance behind the limousines, touching the brake only when drivers ignored his horn.

Blancanales buzzed Lyons. "This is the Pol. We're

going west, staying about a hundred yards behind them.''

''Moving. We'll parallel you, stay out of sight. See anyone interesting?''

''Not really. Over.'' Blancanales watched the vehicles around him. Italian and Japanese compacts zipped in and out of lanes. Buses packed solid with commuters lurched over cracks and potholes in the pavement as men in Levi's and white robes clung to the sides. On one bus, a teenager gripped the front door's handrail while he studied a text with a German title. Faces in the bus windows stared down at Blancanales.

He checked the attaché case beside him. Concealed inside was an Uzi with one hundred fifty rounds of 9mm hollowpoints. The silenced Beretta 93-R rode in an oversize holster under his jacket. He kept his hand radio covered with a map of the city. Blancanales looked up at the faces staring at him, grinned. A small boy grinned back and gave him a two-fingered peace sign.

''Motorcycles are still with the limousines,'' Zaki called back.

Leaning forward, Blancanales saw a teenager behind the Lincolns. Zaki pointed. The other teenager kept his motor scooter behind a Mercedes van, where the limo driver could not spot him in the rearview mirror. The second teenager lifted a walkie-talkie to his lips, spoke a few words, then concealed the radio in a handlebar basket full of books and papers.

Blancanales glanced to both sides, covered his hand radio with his jacket sleeve as he said, ''One of the students on the motorbikes has a radio. I think they're running a pattern behind the limos.'' As Blancanales spoke, a battered and smoking Fiat sedan swerved into the lane. The first motorbike braked, cut across traffic, made a right turn. The motorbike behind the van maintained position.

Two men rode in the front seat of the Fiat. One saw the student on the motorbike, nodded. The student returned the nod.

"They are most definitely running a pattern. Repeat, a pattern. One talked on a radio, a tail car cut in, and the other student dropped out."

"This is the Wizard. I'm finally moving."

"And I'm on some side street," Lyons told them. "Going like crazy."

Traffic slowed as the wide boulevard veered to the northeast. As his taxi pulled up to the bumper of the battered Fiat, Blancanales slid low in the seat. He looked around, saw the student on the motor scooter one lane to his right. Keeping his hand radio below the window level, Blancanales clicked the transmit key twice, then twice again.

"That close?" Lyons asked. "This could get serious."

A Japanese mini-van hit the back bumper of the taxi. Zaki leaned out the window, delivered a curse in Arabic. No one answered. Blancanales looked back and saw the driver leaning through curtains screening the back of the van, speaking to someone.

Visible above the van's dashboard, protruding from a wrapping of newspaper, was a familiar assembly of steel: the front sight and muzzle of a Soviet AKM.

Wrapping the map of Cairo around his hand

radio, Blancanales keyed the transmit. He leaned forward as if questioning the taxi driver. "This is the Politician. Things are now serious. There's a mini-van behind me. Driver's got an AK. The back's curtained off, and he's talking to someone there. This could be a hit squad."

"Think they've spotted you?" Lyons asked.

"They've seen us. We're parked between their cars. But I'm just one more tourist in a taxi."

"Stay with them."

Blancanales laughed. "Can't get away."

A police siren stopped cross traffic. The Cairo PD car led the two Lincoln limousines through the intersection. A wave of buses and trucks and taxis followed. As they accelerated, Blancanales pointed to the right. Zaki saw a gap in the cars and buses and whipped into the space.

The mini-van sped forward. Blancanales watched the driver and windows. The driver kept his eyes on the limousines. The curtained side windows didn't move.

"The van is on our left now. They're closing on the limos."

"I'm buzzing Katz right now," Gadgets answered.

"No!" Lyons broke in. "You'll give us away to the ones that are with him. The CIA and the Egyptian."

"He's got an earphone." Gadgets cut off.

"We're in motion!" Lyons's voice blared out. "Badman to the rescue. . . ."

The shriek of screaming metal, shouts and a blasting horn came through the open channel.

"Are you all right? Sounded like a crash."

"Slow bus, fast taxi," Lyons answered. "But we're gaining fast again. What's going on with the limos?"

"Nothing. The mini-van and the Fiat are closing on them. The kid on the motorcycle's staying back. He's got the radio in his hand. . . ."

Speeding bumper to bumper, the mini-van and the battered sedan approached the limousines. Only a bus separated the limousines from the two pursuing vehicles.

Blancanales leaned forward to Zaki. "Faster. Keep even with them if you can do it."

Zaki saw the curb lane open. He accelerated in a smooth sweep to the right. They passed the teenager on the motor scooter. In his peripheral vision, Blancanales saw the boy lift his walkie-talkie, then they left him behind.

The taxi passed an open-bed cargo truck and a bus. The bus slowed as a passenger stepped off. Zaki whipped the taxi to the left. They came parallel with the mini-van. Blancanales saw a face at a back window watching the traffic. In the front seat of the Fiat, the passenger spoke into a walkie-talkie. The man riding in the back of the mini-van lifted a walkie-talkie to his lips, answered.

Jabbing for the transmit key through the map that wrapped his hand radio, Blancanales shouted, "Wizard! Get Katz moving! They're making their move, they're going to do it!"

Engine screaming, white smoke pouring from the exhaust, the Fiat varoomed to the left, over the center divider. The mini-van followed, horns sounding as the oncoming traffic skidded and swerved around the two wrong-way vehicles. In the instant before the van disappeared behind the bus, the side door flew open. Two men with rocket launchers knelt in the interior.

"RPGs! Wizard, get Katz out!"

In a coordinated maneuver, both Lincolns swerved to the right and hit their brakes, thus putting the bus between them and the hit squad. The Fiat and the van carrying the rocket-launcher team raced into the open but saw no targets. The limousines stopped dead in traffic, tires smoking. Hundreds of tires squealed behind them, bumpers smashed into bumpers, headlights and taillights shattered, horns blared in one vast sound. The police car's siren wailed.

Blancanales flashed past the limousines as Zaki maintained the taxi's speed. They passed the police car. The Fiat and the mini-bus were racing away up the boulevard. Blancanales looked back, saw the limousines accelerate, then skid through a right turn onto a side street.

"Keep that car and van in sight," Blancanales told his driver, then keyed his hand radio. "The limos are safe. We've got the hit team in sight, will follow."

"Plan is to take prisoners, right?" Lyons asked, back in the traffic jam.

"You got it," Blancanales answered.

"Not yet, but give me a minute. . . ."

"What?"

Dropping his hand radio, Lyons leaned forward to his driver. "Abdul, see the kid on the motorbike?"

"Yes, sir. We follow him?"

"For about fifteen seconds."

Two car lengths ahead in the stalled traffic, the

teenager on the motor scooter held the walkie-talkie to his ear. Without uncovering the Atchisson, Lyons grabbed the autoshotgun and the tourist maps covering it, placed it all on the floor of the taxi. Watching the teenager, Lyons checked the Velcro securing the silenced Colt .45 Government Model under his sports coat and waited.

Tires crunched over the broken glass and plastic of the rear-end collisions. The taxi was inching up on the motor scooter. Traffic moved faster as smashed and dented cars, their drivers shouting and waving fists at one another, pulled to the side. Lyons braced himself.

The taxi passed the motor scooter. Lyons waited until the teenager returned the walkie-talkie to his basket, then swung open the door.

In rush-hour traffic, with drivers watching, Lyons threw an arm around the teenager's neck as if he was greeting the boy like a long-lost son. Simultaneously he took hold of the left handlebar. As the boy struggled, Lyons walked the motor scooter to the curb, let it fall and grabbed the walkie-talkie. Choking, kicking, flailing with his fists, the teenager tried to break free. He couldn't. Lyons dragged him into the taxi.

Tires screeched again as the taxi roared away, slicing through traffic.

Lyons keyed his hand radio. "We got one."

5

CLUTCHING A FOLDED-STOCK Kalashnikov rifle, Sadek leaned forward from his rear-facing auxiliary seat. Today, he wore a powder blue summer suit. He lowered the limousine's power window a few inches, observed the traffic behind the limousines. At the other window, Katz held a Colt Commander .45 as he watched parked cars and trucks, bicyclists, sidewalk crowds and vendors flash past. The two Lincolns were careening through the boulevard's traffic.

Parks looked back through the rear window and spoke into the intercom microphone. "We've lost them," he told the chauffeur and the bodyguard in the front seat. "But radio ahead to the airport, tell them to send out an escort car to meet us on the Heliopolis road."

"It is very fortunate you saw them, Mr. Steiner," Sadek said to Katz. Sweat beaded the Egyptian's sharp features. He clicked up the lever safety of the AK. "They were, without a doubt, attempting an assassination."

"You recognize them?" asked Katz, alias Steiner.

"Of course not! Do you mean their nationality? Perhaps Libyans, perhaps radical Palestinians. Foreigners certainly."

"Certainly," Katz agreed. He set the safety of the

Colt, held the autopistol below the level of the window.

"Why not the Brotherhood?" Parks asked.

"Because our security forces broke those fanatics," Sedak pronounced. "However, there are other groups. Foreigners have come to make war in my country. Unfortunate, but true."

"Is it possible your police could capture one of them?" Katz continued in his role of Steiner, speaking English with a slight German accent. "Then we would know...."

"There will be an investigation, have no doubt."

Katz smiled. "I have no doubt."

LOW IN THE BACK SEAT, map wrapping the radio, Blancanales buzzed his partners. Zaki kept the Fiat and mini-van in sight by speeding, then braking, often swerving to maintain his rate through traffic. Horns and screeches came from all sides.

"We're staying behind them. My man's driving like a drunken trucker. But they'll see us gaining on them any second now."

"East on Azhar!" Zaki called back. "They turned east on Sharia el-Azhar."

"Mo-man's moving!" Gadgets's voice told them. "Says we're on...Qua...la.... We're on that street, we turned, we're going north. He says we might make it. Watch them."

"Watching. Making the turn now."

"This is—" Lyons voice came on. Another voice cried out, then Blancanales heard what could only be a fist smashing into flesh, once, twice. "Sorry, but I got a detainee who's acting up. We're right behind you and gaining. Making the turn...."

Looking back, Blancanales saw a taxi take the corner on two wheels. A white-uniformed policeman and many drivers saw the side-slipping taxi approach. The policeman commanded them all to stop with his white-gloved hand. The drivers responded with panic, some hitting their brakes, others standing on their accelerators. Metal smashed, glass fell, another wail of horns began.

Missing one car by inches and losing a taillight to a bus, the taxi then did the impossible: it recovered from the two-wheel turn and sped after Blancanales.

"I do not believe what I just saw. Who do you have driving that car, Ironman?"

"Man, this is wild. Here we come. I'll take point, you fall back. We'll rotate with the Wizard, chase these freaks wherever they go. But lose them or not, we got this prisoner."

As he listened, Blancanales saw the taxi carrying Lyons pass. Lyons gave him a salute. Ahead, the cars of the hit team made another right turn.

"Wizard. They went right."

"We got them, got them!" Mohammed the driver laughed, leaned on his horn, stood on the accelerator, whipped to the left and braked. As the taxi slowed to a roll behind a truck, Mohammed leaned out the window and squinted into the fading light. "They're up there, but I don't see them."

"Think we can get close?" Gadgets asked him. "Close enough to slap a magnetic DF on them?"

Mohammed turned his head and gave a manic grin, his long, oval face and white teeth glowing with mischief. "Oh, yeahhhhhhh."

They passed a park of palms and yellow dust. Mohammed eased through traffic as Gadgets scanned the street and the parkways. On the broad tree-shaded walkways, artisans and vendors bustled past old men on benches. Schoolchildren crowded around a skateboard. Then Gadgets caught a glimpse of traffic beyond the walkways.

"Stop here," he told Mohammed. "Wait for me."

Dodging through idle taxis and the vendors' carts, Gadgets pressed through the mob. Several wide walk-ways converged at a monument. He saw another street, more parked taxis and buses, more vendors. The street curved around the park to create a crescent-shaped island of walkways and gardens. He looked for the Fiat sedan or the mini-van that Blancanales had described. He didn't see them, and he turned back.

Out of nowhere, a mini-van screeched to a stop. Gadgets stood still in the walking crowd and watched two men slam open the side door. A Fiat double-parked next to the mini-van. The driver and passenger left the Fiat to unlock the doors of a nearby step-up van. Moving across the paved path, Gadgets kept his eyes away from the terrorist crew, watched them with his peripheral vision as he let the flow of pedestrians carry him toward the curb. The sun was low in the sky, the day still blazing bright but cooler at last.

Stepping into the street, he slipped the DF from his pocket. He eased to the side for a moment, giving way to a knot of laughing teenagers. He pressed the mag-net against the van's sheet metal, felt it click tight. He heard voices in the truck behind him.

He walked behind the truck to see two men transfer-ring burlap-wrapped bundles from the van to the truck. The bundles were the size and shape of RPG-7 rocket launchers. Two newspaper-wrapped rifles followed. Gadgets continued past the double-parked van, then hurried behind another truck. Almost running, he rushed through the crowded park, shoved past two vendors who had spotted him as a tourist, jumped in his waiting taxi.

Jamming down his radio's transmit key, he ducked down low to watch the walkways. Mohammed swerved into traffic. "This is the Wizard. I got the DF on them, quick and dirty. Saw them changing cars. Took a light blue step-up van, don't know what. Got Arabic writing on the side in white letters—"

Lyons's voice cut him off. "We're at the north end of the street, going slow."

On the boulevard, Blancanales keyed his hand radio as Zaki pulled their cab to the curb. "We're parked. If they double back, we'll be here. When they move, keep your distance. They got rockets."

"I saw them get into the van," Gadgets confirmed.

"There they are," Lyons told his partners. "They're going—going east. Politician, go! Wizard, catch up and take over! I'll circle around the park."

Zaki rolled into the flow of traffic three vehicles behind the blue step van. As the bright afternoon suddenly became gloomy dusk, with a swiftness common to Cairo's latitude, lights came on, and the dust and diesel smoke from the boulevards drifted around the neon signs like fog. Blancanales located the DF receiver in his attaché case and flicked the power switch. A loud, steady drone came from the unit.

His hand radio buzzed. "Wizard here. Coming up behind you."

Blancanales turned down the volume of his DF receiver and checked the map covering his radio. "We're with them. Tried the DF; it's strong."

A horn honked outside Blancanales's window. Gadgets waved from the back of the taxi as he passed. His voice came from the hand radio. "Now I'm point."

"You got it. Watch for rockets. Crazy man back there. How's your prisoner?"

"Alive. No identification. Old Welby .38 revolver. Radio's a cheapie, held together with sealing tape. Whoever they are, they aren't well financed."

"Spent all their money on rifles and rocket-propelled grenades," Blancanales muttered.

"We checked the park. The Fiat and the van are still there—must be stolen."

Gadgets monitored the conversation as his driver followed the van. Only two passenger sedans separated them. He leaned forward to Mohammed. "A little more distance...."

"Where we taking this punk for interrogation?" Lyons asked. "You appreciate we cannot put the questions to him in hotel rooms."

His driver, Abdul, answered. "There is a place available. The colonel did not intend you to return to the hotels. Your registration was only to satisfy the authorities' expectations."

"Maybe we should take this one there and dump him."

A motor scooter backfired next to the taxi. Lyons started, instinctively reaching for the pistol under his sports coat. He saw a teenager on a motor scooter looking at him. Then the boy accelerated off between two cars.

Lyons buzzed his partner. "Pol, you said they had two kids on motorbikes?"

"One took off, one stayed on. I guess that's the one you got...."

"The other one's coming up. He eyeballed me, then kept going."

Now the popping and backfiring of the scooter came from the lane next to Blancanales. He kept his head turned away but knew the boy had seen him. "Zaki, that motor scooter next to us...."

"It is one of them. He looked at us."

Blancanales slipped out his silenced Beretta 93-R. He touched the extractor to confirm the round in the chamber, then thumbed back the hammer and set the safety. He looked up to see the teenager two lengths ahead, steering the scooter with one hand, holding a walkie-talkie to his mouth with the other.

Blancanales spoke quickly in his own radio. "Wizard, you heard. That kid's got to fall."

"Unnecessary. They're looking for you, not me. So just stay back, let the Ironman and me switch off the tag car. With a DF and three cars, we can't lose. There goes the kid, he's eyeballing everybody, looking for surveillance. They can't dodge every cab in the city. I say we just hang loose, play it cool."

"Yeah, man," Mohammed agreed from the front seat. "We're too cool."

Ahead of the taxi, a car changed lanes to the right, a truck to the left. Only asphalt separated them from the step van of terrorists. The motor scooter sputtered in the lane to their right. Mohammed sped ahead to the bumper of the van.

"We're too cool, no one would *think* of messing

with us.'' Mohammed slapped the steering wheel to a beat only he heard. ''Too cool, too cool.''

''Hey, driver. Act natural! That kid's looking at us.''

Mohammed turned to face Gadgets. ''Dig it, dude. I was born here. I know what is natural.''

The van's doors flew open. Even as Mohammed turned forward again, Gadgets threw himself over him and jerked the wheel sharply to the right. The taxi sideswiped another taxi, both cars sliding sideways. Mohammed saw an RPG pointed at him from the back of the van. He floored the accelerator, jammed the steering wheel to the left, then spun it to the right.

Falling over the seat back into the front seat, Gadgets looked up at the side wall of the van. He pulled out his silenced Beretta. Mohammed slammed back the transmission lever, the engine shrieked with red-line rpm in low gear. The rear tires flattened as they bit for purchase near the van's right side door.

The pointed nose of an RPG-7 emerged from that door.

''Lean back—don't move!'' Gadgets screamed at Mohammed.

He double-actioned the first shot of a three-round burst.

Flame flashed as the gunner fired the rocket.

6

THE FLASH lit up the pollution gray of the Cairo dusk.

Blancanales saw a point of flame streak away into the sky, then explode. Zaki floored the car through traffic, came to a taxi stalled sideways in a lane and pulled up behind the step van. Flames rose from the van's doors.

"Wizard! What...." Blancanales shouted into his hand radio.

"They tried to hit us with a rocket. I shot first. We're past them, making distance. What do you see?"

"The van's burning. Zaki, what do you say we play concerned citizens? Try to help those—"

"Others are. Look."

"We're getting out to take a look."

Lyons skidded to a stop one lane to the left. Behind them, a thousand horns blared. Lyons leaned from his window and called across to his partner, "I got a prisoner to sit on, so I'll watch the cabs."

Blancanales left his taxi. Both their drivers, Abdul and Zaki, charged into the smoke and confusion. Blancanales jerked the step van's back doors open, ducked down to avoid any shots. None came. He looked inside, saw flames and black smoke churning from the foam plastic of the driver's seat. The driver burned with the seat. A second dead man sprawled on the floor of the van, an RPG launcher still in his hands. A screaming man clawed at the van's sheet-metal floor, dragging himself away from the heat of the flames. Smoke rose from the man's flesh and clothes.

Blancanales knew what had happened. He had seen a People's Army of Vietnam soldier inadvertently killed when the backblast of a rocket launcher hit him. The Muslim terrorists had fired the RPG-7 inside the closed van, and the rocket blast had hit the driver point-blank and seared the other man.

"Abdul! Zaki! Back here!" Blancanales called out, then climbed into the van. He grabbed the hand of the burned man to pull him away from the flames.

The seared skin of the man's hand came away like a glove. Blancanales grabbed him by the belt, dragged him to the back of the van. Abdul and Zaki lowered the guy to the pavement.

In the glare of the taxi's headlights, the terrorist's horrible burns made the onlookers gasp. The rocket flame had melted his eyes and features, reduced his flesh to cooked meat covered with the ashes of his shirt and coat. He waved his hands above him, groping for light, not yet understanding his loss of vision.

"To the hospital!" Blancanales called out to the two drivers.

Abdul shouted out in Arabic to the onlookers. Several men in the crowd helped lift the burned terrorist from the asphalt and gently carry him to Blancanales's taxi. They eased him onto the back seat.

Blancanales jumped into the front as Zaki gunned the engine. Zaki leaned on the horn. Abdul and

Lyons followed in their taxi. They heard approaching sirens as they left the flames of the scene behind.

"Two prisoners," Blancanales radioed Gadgets.

"That man isn't going to live," Lyons added. "If we're going to get anything out of him, it's got to be quick."

Zaki turned to Blancanales. "The colonel anticipated prisoners. There is a place ready."

"Take us there."

After five minutes of speeding through the labyrinth of Cairo's streets, Blancanales saw Mohammed and Gadgets pushing up a rolling steel door. The roar of engines, the clanging of hammers on steel filled the area with noise. Blancanales looked around at the narrow street of auto and welding shops, saw white flashes of torches lighting the interiors, then his taxi followed Gadgets into a warehouse. Lyons and Abdul screeched to a stop behind them a second later. Mohammed pulled down the door.

Bare light bulbs lit the oily, soot-fouled interior. While their drivers checked the shadows and corners of the building for any possible intruders, Able Team pulled the burned terrorist from the taxi.

"How'd this happen to him?" Lyons asked.

"Remember when they trained you with the RPG-7, they told you to keep clear of the backblast?" Gadgets reminded him. "When I shot the one with the RPG, this one must've caught the backblast."

"He caught part of it," Blancanales corrected. "The driver got most of it. Killed him."

"That's why Stony Man sent us those German rockets," Gadgets added. "You can fire an Armburst out of your coat pocket—"

"Get some morphine, Gadgets," Blancanales interrupted as he leaned over the charred terrorist. "Trunk of my cab. Lyons, we aren't going to get anything out of this guy. He's in shock and dying. Listen to his breathing. I'd say his mouth and throat are burned bad. Maybe his lungs."

"Don't give him the morphine yet.... Abdul! Over here."

"Yes, sir."

Lyons went to their taxi, pulled the semiconscious teenage terrorist from the car floor. He and Abdul sat the punk down on oil-black concrete away from the other prisoner. Lyons slapped the terrorist, grabbed him by the hair, pounded his head against the taxi's fender. The boy's eyes opened.

"Tell him he is a prisoner. Tell him if he cooperates, he lives. If he doesn't, we torture him until he does."

Abdul translated. The boy shook his head. Abdul spoke to him, the boy answering with a few words. He closed his eyes, mumbled words.

"He's praying. He says he fights for Allah. The Brotherhood preaches that if their fighters die, they ascend to heaven to stand at the right hand of Allah."

"So he wants to be a martyr?"

Abdul nodded.

"Ask him what kind of martyrdom he wants."

Hearing the translated words of the American in front of him, the boy cried out, struggled against the plastic handcuffs looped around his wrists and ankles. Lyons slammed a fist into the terrorist's ribs, doubling him over. The boy's breathing came in sobs as Lyons grabbed him by the arms and dragged him around the taxi.

"Tell him he'll talk, or we'll do *this* to him...."

As Abdul translated again, Lyons dumped the boy next to the other prisoner, shoved the boy's face to the blinded, disfigured, dying man.

The boy screamed, thrashed. Lyons held him by the hair and the shirt collar, kept his face only inches from the horror.

"Will he talk now? Ask him!"

The boy nodded.

A GATE OF CORRUGATED STEEL ten feet high slid aside for the limousines and escort car. In the blue white glare of mercury arc lights, crew-cut young Americans in uniforms without insignia, M-16 rifles in their hands, watched the Lincolns enter. While the others stayed back, one soldier advanced to the first limousine and motioned for the driver to roll down the window. The soldier glanced at the driver and bodyguard in the front seat, then at the CIA passengers. He repeated the procedure with the second limousine, waving a flashlight over the faces of Katz, Sadek and Parks. The limousines continued to the hangars. The escort car, a mid-seventies Dodge with a full-powered engine and heavy-duty suspension, parked near the soldiers.

Katz glanced back, saw soldiers searching the interior and trunk of the Dodge. The three CIA soldiers left the car and stood to one side.

"We're on full alert," Parks explained. "Marines will search these cars when we park. Can't be too careful."

"Someone was not careful last night," Katz commented.

"And he died."

"True. But the death of Mr. Hershey does not solve the failure of the security of this facility."

"It took the Muslims a year to infiltrate our operation. It'll take time to find—"

"Mr. Parks," Katz corrected him, "you don't have time."

The limousines came to a stop. Parks opened the door. He stepped into the cool wind and squinting against the blowing dust, held the door open for Katz and Sadek.

"I know I don't have the time. I know it. But you can't expect me to take over the station one night and break a major terrorist operation the next day. Let's see what the electronics crew came up with. . . ."

As the three men crossed the asphalt to the door of the hangar's office, Katz, limping slightly as always, touched the tiny hearing aid behind his ear. He smiled at what he heard.

Technicians saluted Parks as he entered the office. "We found no micro-transmitters or com-line interceptions, sir. We found nothing at all."

A STREET OF WHITEWASHED SHOPS glowed with the soft colors of a theater's neon. Crowding around the entrance, teenagers waved tickets at a fat man. Other teenagers left the theater, boys punching and shoving one another. Abdul and Lyons rolled through the intersection.

Lyons pointed to the crowd. "What's going on there? Politics?"

Abdul glanced at the marquee. "Bruce Lee."

Smiling, Lyons checked his modified Colt. He undid his belt, secured several mag pouches. His hand radio buzzed. It was Schwarz.

"News from Katz, Ironman. Air force technicians have swept the hangars, telephone lines, the perimeter. No electronics."

"Talk show's over," Lyons said. "We're at the alley. On our way in...."

Abdul parked the taxi. Then he slid an Uzi from under his seat and followed Lyons into a narrow alley. Lights behind sooty windows cast no illumination into the narrow corridor of shadow and filth. Above them, voices screamed from tenements. Radio songs in the strange chromatic scale of Arabia drifted down. Lyons pulled back the hammer of his .45, held the silenced autopistol ready.

He heard Abdul's steps behind him. Lyons slowed as he came to a tangle of trash. A faint light revealed a twisted length of steel jutting from a building. At six feet above the paving stones, it posed no danger to Egyptians. Lyons memorized the position of the hazard. If he had to run out of the alley, he didn't want the angle iron to take off the top of his head.

"Two more doors," Abdul whispered.

Silently, Lyons slid out his hand radio. Abdul went to the door. Lyons clicked the radio's transmit key, once, then three times. He repeated the code, heard Blancanales and Gadgets acknowledge with clicks. He returned the radio to the flap pocket and checked the Atchisson slung on his back. No tangles, no hang-ups.

Abdul eased the door open. Dry hinges creaked. A low voice challenged him from inside.

Answering in quick Arabic, Abdul stepped back, putting the Uzi behind his back. A flashlight splashed light into the alley. Lyons watched as the muzzle of an AK appeared, then the shadowy form of the sentry holding the autorifle and flashlight.

A .45 slug exploded the silhouette's skull as Lyons shoved the AK muzzle aside. The sentry died before he could jerk the rifle's trigger. Lyons covered the narrow passage leading into the tenement as Abdul concealed the corpse.

They slipped inside and eased the door closed. Lyons took out his radio again. He pulled out the tiny earphones, plugged it into his ear, keyed the transmit.

"Wizard, Pol. Sentries. Hold where you are. We'll clear those street doors for you."

Clicks acknowledged.

Lyons crept through the darkness, feeling his way with his feet. Both his hands were on the Colt. The fire selector was set on burst. The old floor of the tenement vibrated with footsteps above them. A radio voice wailed. They followed the passage past two bricked-up doorways. Finally, a wood-plank door stopped them. Lyons and Abdul waited, listened. They heard only the radio. Abdul pointed to himself as he reached for the handle.

Steel scraped on concrete, the door flew open, knocking Abdul back. A form pushed through the doorway. Lyons saw the outline of a slung rifle. He fired.

Three .45 slugs slammed the terrorist sideways, fragments of skull and brain raining down in the passage. Lyons looked away from the headless corpse, saw a second shadow in the doorway.

A voice screamed in Arabic. Three hollowpoint slugs smashed into the terrorist's chest, the impact driving out his last word in an explosion of breath and blood. The Colt's slide locked back.

Lyons's earphone buzzed, the voice of Blancanales blasting directly into his ear, the words shouted, desperate, "Lyons! Lyons! They—"

The voice cut off. Something had happened out front. But Lyons could do nothing to help his partners.

Feet pounded on steel steps. Dropping the magazine with one hand, Lyons snatched a second from his belt. He jammed in the load of seven 190-grain hollowpoints, then glanced around the corner.

A group of young men were crowding down the stairs. One had an old submachine gun, the others knives. Lyons sighted on the one with the autoweapon, put a slug into his heart. The impact threw the dead teenager against the others. They grabbed him, didn't see Lyons as he stepped out in a combat crouch to sight on them. Lurching and spinning with the impacts, the other three fell dead or dying. Lyons watched the shadows above the stairs. He pulled out his radio with his left hand.

More feet rang on the stairs. In a suicidal rush, a wild-eyed old mullah with an AK threw himself at the American. Lyons looked into the 7.62mm bore of the autoweapon. He brought his .45 Colt Commander on line. His finger touched the trigger an instant too late.

7

MEANWHILE, at the curb in front of the tenement, Gadgets and Mohammed scanned the street for sentries. At the far end of the block, a man in ragged polyester pants and jacket stood in the door of a café. But he did not watch the street. He argued with someone inside, violently gesturing with his arms, then staggered away, weaving with drunkenness.

A car door closed. Gadgets glanced back, saw Blancanales leave his taxi. He saw no one else on the dark street.

"The trunk."

As if helping a tourist, Mohammed hurried to the back of the Fiat and snapped open the trunk. Gadgets reached inside, took an Armburst rocket, slung it over his shoulder. Mohammed whistled softly. "Man, you're going to do it to them."

"Before they do it to me."

Voices shattered the silence of the dark street.

Gadgets reached into the back seat and snatched up the Uzi. He concealed it under his coat. Mohammed followed a step behind him as Gadgets hurried into the shadows.

Two young men came around the corner. They crossed the street to enter the café. Gadgets looked in the other direction. He saw Blancanales leave a door-way.

The radio in Gadgets's coat pocket clicked. The code meant Lyons had reached the alley door. Gadgets acknowledged, then signaled Blancanales. He left his concealment and walked silently along the shuttered shop fronts. Mohammed followed him. He, too, was concealing an Uzi under his cabdriver's jacket.

They stopped at double-wide doors of heavy planks. Light shone through the cracks. Inside, voices spoke in Arabic. A radio blared. Blancanales stood at the other side of the door and looked up at the windows and balconies hanging over the street.

Light came from a window on the second floor. Blancanales slung his Uzi over his back, then checked the holster of the silenced Beretta under his sports coat. He found handholds in the old bricks and eased himself up the wall. He worked the toes of his shoes into the cracks between the bricks.

Gadgets slipped out his Beretta and thumbed back the hammer. Blancanales reached the window and climbed to the side of it, searching for firm hand-holds and toeholds. He peered into the room. He snapped his head back suddenly, went flat against the wall. Gadgets brought up the Beretta.

A bearded old frizzy-haired man leaned out the window, looking in both directions on the street. He did not see Blancanales. The old man returned to the interior of the room. Blancanales peered in again. He waited a few seconds, then crawled through the window.

"A mullah..." Mohammed whispered.

Lyons's voice spoke from their hand radios. "Wizard, Pol. Sentries. Hold where you are. We'll clear those street doors for you."

Someone in the room heard Blancanales's radio. From the street, Gadgets saw a sports coat fly open, then heard the slap of a suppressed slug hitting flesh. Then silence.

Blancanales leaned out of the window. He waved to Gadgets.

Gadgets clicked an acknowledgment to Lyons. Above him, Blancanales signaled for Gadgets to wait.

Yellow sputters from a kerosene lantern lighted the room. The old mullah sprawled against the wall. A Kalashnikov rifle lay beyond the reach of his dead hand. Blancanales crept across the room, the floor-boards creaking under his weight. He heard footsteps outside the door.

A voice called quietly in Arabic. Blancanales froze. He swore at his ignorance of the language. If he could understand the words, if he could fake an answer. . . .

Knuckles tapped the door. Two knocks, three knocks. The door's handle rattled. Blancanales tiptoed behind the door. A band of light from the other room expanded as the door opened. A teenager with a cap over his curly hair leaned into the room. The boy saw the feet of the old man and entered.

Blancanales sent a slug through the base of the boy's skull. He looked into the lighted room. Parts of a field-stripped AK covered a table. He saw an RPG-7 rocket launcher propped against the wall. He entered the room, the Beretta ready, pivoted slowly to scan every corner.

Screams! Running feet! Weapons clattered, doors flew open. Voices called to one another.

Blancanales grabbed his hand radio. "Lyons! Lyons! They—"

A robed man shoved back through the door that the others had fled through. His eyes went wide when he saw the American with the pistol. Blancanales put a burst in the man's face.

He peered through the door and saw a long hallway. At one end, a white-robed man clutched an AK. Wide-eyed with fear, the old man stared around him, shrieked at the sight of Blancanales, dashed down a flight of steel stairs.

A silent .45-caliber slug slammed into the ceiling of the hallway. As a body thumped down stairs, Blancanales heard shrieking and the clanging of steel on steel. He rushed to the stairway, stayed out of the line of fire. Blood dripped from the whitewashed walls.

"Ironman! You okay?"

"Yeah, yeah. I even got a prisoner. I tell you, this is strictly amateur night...."

Blancanales buzzed Gadgets. "Action in here. What's going on out there?"

"Nothing. Absolute zero. What happened?"

"Tell you later."

Stepping over corpses as he rushed down the stairs, Blancanales saw Lyons standing over the mullah, one foot on the old man's throat, the modified Colt Government Model pointed at his face. The mullah choked, thrashed, raised a clawlike hand for mercy. The other arm lay limp at his side, the shoulder shattered, blood from the gaping wound soaking his white robe.

"With losers like these against us," Lyons sneered, "we'll be going home tonight. He had me. In his sights. And look...."

He pointed the Colt at the AK. The autorifle had no magazine in place. "Tried to shoot me with an empty gun. Abdul. Watch this lowlife."

The breathless taxi driver stood over the prisoner as Lyons looped plastic handcuffs around the old man's wrists and cinched them tight. He fitted two of the plastic locking strips end to end and bound the prisoner's ankles. Finally, he tore a shirt from one of the dead teenagers and wadded it into the mullah's mouth.

Silenced autopistol pointed, Lyons followed the passage toward the street. At the far end, a single bare bulb illuminated the long narrow passage. They stopped at a door. Lyons nodded at the light, looked at the Beretta that Blancanales held. Blancanales sighted on the bulb and popped it with a slug.

In the darkness, a fine line of light outlined the door. Lyons crouched beside the door. Blancanales flattened himself against the wall near the handle. Lyons jerked the door open, dodged back behind the cover of the wall.

No shots came. They heard no movement. Keeping his head low, at less than knee height, below the point where a terrorist inside would aim a burst of autofire, Lyons stuck his head out for a look, saw a garage cluttered with auto parts and tools and jerked his head back.

"Don't see anyone...."

"Doesn't mean they don't see you," Blancanales whispered. He took out his hand radio to buzz Gadgets. "Wizard. Hit that door, make noise, a distraction. On the count of three."

"Got it. One, two. . . ."

On three, bursts of silent 9mm slugs hammered into the ceiling and rear wall of the garage, a fender crashing down, glass breaking, plaster falling. Lyons slid belly-down through the doorway.

He saw no one. Staying on the floor, Lyons braced the Colt with both hands. Rolling on his back, he peered into every corner of the garage.

Gadgets knocked on the heavy doors, hissed, "The kid on the motorbike's coming." Then Lyons's hand radio buzzed. He did not stop to answer it as he pulled the crossbar from the doors.

Blancanales leaned through the doorway. "Wizard says the kid on the motorcycle's coming. Thinks you should let him in. . . ."

"Already. . . ." Lyons cut off his answer as the two-stroke roar of the motor scooter became deafening. He stayed behind the door as he pulled it open. The teenager rode in on his Japanese bike.

Three pistols and an Uzi greeted him, Gadgets and Mohammed rushing in a step behind the teenage terrorist. Lyons shoved the door closed. In seconds, they had the boy gagged and bound.

"Back to the stairway?" said Lyons.

Rejoining Abdul, Lyons and Blancanales looked up the stairway to the tenement apartments.

Blancanales shook his head. "I don't want to chance it. There could be a hundred of them up there. Waiting with AKs."

"Second the motion," Lyons agreed. "Maybe they control the entire building, maybe not. There could be children, old people on the upper floors. Depends on what raghead here tells us.''

As Blancanales surveyed the stairway, he took a mental body count. "Five. Plus three more upstairs...."

"And two more there.'' Lyons pointed toward the alley. He held up his suppressed autopistol. "Colt seven, Beretta three. Winner and still champion...."

Stepping past the door, Blancanales looked down at the sentry. One slug had smashed the left arm where it met the shoulder. The arm dangled by tendons and strands of muscle. Only the jaw and a scrap of scalp remained of the head. Blancanales exhaled slowly.

"That's an example of burst fire,'' Lyons told him. "Point-blank.''

"Let's get this old man into the garage.'' Blancanales handed his Beretta and an extra fifteen-round magazine to Abdul and left him at the stairs.

They dragged the mullah over the stones. In the garage, Mohammed questioned the mullah. The old man babbled, nodded his head, cried.

"If we let him live,'' Mohammed told them, "he'll tell us everything, take us to the others.''

"He doesn't want to be a martyr?'' Lyons sneered.

"That's only for soldiers,'' Mohammed grinned. "This old man, when he dies, he knows where he goes.''

"Do they have more SAM-7 missiles?'' Lyons asked. Blancanales spoke simultaneously.

"How do they get their information about the planes?''

Mohammed translated their questions, listened to

the old man whine and cry. "He wants you to stop the pain in his shoulder."

Lyons looked at the two prisoners, then motioned Blancanales and Gadgets to the passage door. There, Lyons glanced down to the stairway to check on Abdul. He watched the passage as the three men talked in whispers.

"I don't think he's the head man," Blancanales told them. "The old man upstairs had a servant, and he had better robes."

"But he's dead," Lyons commented. He called over to Mohammed. "Ask him if he's the leader, the number one man."

When Mohammed questioned the mullah, the old man nodded again and again, looking around at his captors, beseeching them with his one hand. Mohammed shook his head. "Says he is, but he ain't. I say he's a stupid old priest from the desert."

"Does he know where the missiles are?" Lyons asked.

For minutes, Mohammed translated questions and answers. "He says there are missiles someplace else. If you stop the pain, get him to a doctor, he'll take you there. He doesn't know anything about the airport. Doesn't know anything about the CIA. His group makes war on America. That's all he knows."

"Pushing our luck," Gadgets told them. "We go to another place, and they're ready for us...."

"I haven't seen any telephones or radios," Blancanales told them.

"They have walkie-talkies," Gadgets cautioned. "Limited range, but...."

"This isn't their main group," Lyons reasoned.

"That old man, he's no one. Not these punks, either. They had old AKs and pistols and knives. You see the submachine gun that one raghead punk had? Looked like something out of World War II. They wouldn't have the missiles here. The main group would. When we get *them*, that's when this show's over."

"That's what that Hershey goof thought," Gadgets muttered. "And now he's over."

"Hershey had a traitor or informer in his team for sure," Blancanales corrected. "We don't."

"Gentlemen—" Lyons numbered his points "—one: we came in here quick and quiet. No shots. No warning. Two: no one got out. Therefore, I vote we hit the next group."

"Second the motion," Blancanales agreed.

"It's unanimous, then. Let's hit them. But," Gadgets cautioned Lyons, "what you mean is, no one got out that you know of.... Now they could be expecting us, right?"

Lyons nodded.

8

THE NEON LIGHTS advertised cafés and restaurants. Groups of well-dressed men stood on the sidewalks. In the back seat of a taxi, Lyons and Mohammed held the bleeding mullah between them as they surveyed the street. Lyons watched the sidewalks, the open eateries, the countless Egyptians enjoying an early-evening coffee or dinner, but he knew he would not spot sentries. Anyone could be a sentry. Sentries could be watching from the rooftops of the apartments.

Lyons saw taxis carrying tourists weave through the traffic and the double-parked autos.

So it works both ways, he thought. *We can't spot them, maybe they can't spot us. Maybe.*

"There, that place," Mohammed translated, looking at a café crowded with students and young professionals. Lounging in wicker chairs around small tables, the young men drank coffee from tiny cups. Groups talked, some argued, others read newspapers.

"That's a hangout for fanatics?"

"Garages in back. He says there's an alley. The organization has all the rooms upstairs. A whole lot of dudes up there."

"Where are the missiles?"

"He just says, 'In there, in there.' I don't think he really knows."

"But that's the place?"

"That's what he says."

"He dies if he's lying."

"Oh, yeah. He knows."

Lyons leaned forward. "Abdul, go around the corner slow. I want to look down that alley."

Abdul nodded, eased the taxi through the pedestrians cutting across the street. He stopped as a middle-aged blond man and woman jaywalked in front of him. Horns sounded behind the taxi.

"Tourists," Abdul commented as he rolled through a right turn. As if searching for an address, he peered at the small shops and apartment entries.

Lyons saw a wide commercial alley. Lights illuminated service entries and parked trucks. On the higher floors, balconies jutted from the back walls of the buildings.

"I know how we're going in," Lyons muttered.

"Should've scoped out your partner making like Spiderman," Mohammed told him. "For an old guy, he does all right."

Lyons laughed. "We'll see how you do, kiddo."

"Not me, man. I'll take the escalator."

"And ride straight into a kill zone."

"Never happen. I'm too cool. I'm telepathic. I can see into the future...."

"Oh, yeah?" Lyons continued laughing. "What do you see for tonight?"

"Dead people, man. Dead people."

"Who?"

Mohammed laughed, put out his palm. "Five dollars, I tell your fortune. I tell you who dies."

"Why pay? I'll find out soon enough."

A BEEPING came from the belt of Sadek's tailored slacks. He touched his pager, smiled to Parks and Katz.

"Excuse me, my friends. This marvelous American invention tells me I must call my office." His smile dropped. Unclipping the tiny box of electronics, he looked at it, held it up to the other men. "If Allah had seen fit that this did not function, if I had not responded so quickly to our friend Hershey's call, perhaps he would have forestalled his unfortunate venture. The irony.... Forgive me, I return immediately."

Katz watched the Egyptian liaison officer cross the vast concrete-and-steel vault of the hangar. Speaking for an instant with a soldier, Sadek went to a noncom's desk, dialed a number.

"Does he know of the flight?" Katz-alias-Steiner asked Parks.

"Mr. Steiner, I did as you asked. He doesn't know. But let me tell you, Sadek isn't the spy. He didn't have to help Hershey. He ran out in that street. My men didn't have the guts to do what he did. He's a good man, a professional. Being an Egyptian doesn't make him a fanatic."

Across the hangar, Sadek took notes from what he heard on the telephone. Katz calculated the cost of the Egyptian secret police officer's fashionable suit, his English wing tips, the gold wristwatch. The CIA file on Sadek described him as the only son of an alcoholic poet. Though his father died early, the boy had not suffered. His wealthy relatives showered money and gifts on him. His father's older brother had paid for private schools in Egypt, then English universities. Another uncle held open a vice-presidency in the family's lucrative import concern for the time when the young officer retired from government service.

"If I had not read his dossier," Katz commented, "I would question how a civil servant could live as he does."

"I went to his grandfather's estate. For a high society reception. The man doesn't have to work. He works because he wants to serve his country and his people. Save your time, don't even bother investigating him. I trust the man with my life."

AS THE TAXI ROLLED TO A STOP at a restaurant's service entrance, four men stepped out and slipped into the shadows. The taxi pulled away and disappeared into traffic. Surrounded by barrels of garbage and trash, the three Americans and their driver looked like wandering tourists. Their sports coats concealed their radios and shoulder-holstered autopistols. Mohammed concealed an Uzi and several mags in an equipment bag. They carried no other gear or weapons.

Without a word, Lyons led them through the alley's darkness. He pointed to a truck, then to the apartment balconies above the alley. The apartments had European-style fire escapes, the steel landings doubling as balconies. Flowerpots and planter boxes covered the landings. The other men nodded. Lyons stepped up onto the parked truck's bumper and climbed to the top of the cargo van. He tested the ladder, then went up quickly, his neoprene-soled shoes silent on the rungs.

Glancing into the lighted interior of the second-floor apartment as he passed, he saw a middle-aged man and woman watching a black-and-white television. He continued up. In the next apartment, two teenage girls danced to a loud Elvis Presley song. The girls whirled and spun like bobby-soxers in an old American Bandstand show.

Lyons stopped on the last rungs to scan the rooftop. He saw vent pipes and antennas silhouetted against the distant lights of high-rise towers. But Lyons could see nothing in the darkness of the black tar roof. He snaked over the top, crouching in the darkness.

He unhooked his hand radio from his belt. "I'm on top. Waiting for you." Then Lyons spoke to Zaki in the taxi waiting on a side street. They had sent Abdul back to the garage to dump the prisoners. "Taximan. You monitoring?"

"Yes, sir. I'm parked and monitoring."

"When Abdul gets back, have him wait where you left us. Understand?"

"Yes, sir."

The steel ladder vibrated with steps. In seconds, Blancanales swung over the wall, followed by Gadgets and Mohammed. Waiting for their eyes to adjust, they listened. City noises and snatches of music came from the streets below. A ventilator fan grated in its housing. The smells of cooking oils and cigarettes swirled around them. After a minute, they could see gray shapes and the lines of wires within the darkness.

Moving again, Lyons crouchwalked toward the roof of the adjoining building. He felt his way past the guy wires of antennas, his eyes continuously sweeping the shadows and forms ahead of him for the movement of a sentry. He heard only the faint cracking of dust and grit under his shoes.

At the edge of the roof, Lyons waited again as the three shadows caught up with him. They peered over the low wall to the next building. A stereo played loudly beneath them. The roof vibrated with the beat of the music.

The bricks of the two apartment buildings met. There was no airspace or easement between the walls. Scanning the next roof, Able Team and friend saw another expanse of shadows and darkness. The captured mullah had told them that the next building over housed the Muslim Brotherhood group.

"There has to be someone standing guard up here," Blancanales whispered to Lyons.

"That old man jived us," Gadgets grunted.

"Maybe." Lyons gouged a bit of asphalt from the roof, flicked it.

A dog barked, once, twice, then went quiet. They heard the feet of other dogs running across the roof, then more barking. The dogs whined, became silent.

Lyons tapped Blancanales and Gadgets. "I'm making a noise on the far side, then we go over. Berettas...."

Searching through the darkness with his fingers, Lyons found another hunk of asphalt. To avoid silhouetting himself against the sky, he crept over the roof to a fan housing and stood up with the bulk of the housing behind him. He watched the far building for almost a minute. Watching for movement. Then he hissed to the others and heaved the asphalt high over the rooftops.

The four men went over the low wall and ran

across baked asphalt and sheet metal to the far side of the apartment building. The dogs barked. A voice shouted. Lyons saw his partners and Mohammed slink away through the antennas and vents. A tangle of barbed wire stopped them.

Barking continued on the opposite side of the roof. The four men spread out along the fence of planks and barbed wire. They knew the security fence would have gates. The group inside the building would have provided for rooftop escape.

Blancanales went slowly, feeling ahead of him for booby traps or noise-making trash. He peered up at the barbed wire, then moved along, fingers sweeping over the gritty surface. He found a bottle, then another, set them far to the side. His fingers found something soft, coarse, like burlap. He felt the shape of it. A dead rat.

He set the stiff, sun-dried rodent where he could find it, resumed his search for the gate. He located a loop of chain and a lock that secured a rectangle of old lumber set between two planks. Crawling backward, he picked up the rat, went back to Gadgets.

"Gate's down there," Blancanales whispered, his mouth close enough to touch Gadgets's hair. "It's got a lock."

"On my way. Two clicks on the radio when you want me to open the gate."

Blancanales continued to Lyons and Mohammed. "The Wizard'll open the gate. . . ."

The creaking of a door stopped his whisper. Footsteps crossed the roof. The three men froze in their crouches as the footsteps passed on the other side of the low wall. While the dogs continued barking, the sentry walked a circuit of the other rooftop. A voice shouted in Arabic at the dogs. The dogs trailed off, then one dog barked again, then all the dogs joined in. The sentry shouted once more. A bottle broke. The dogs scattered, finally went quiet.

The footsteps returned to the stairwell, and the door creaked closed. Footsteps went down stairs.

"Give the Wizard two clicks," Blancanales whispered. "I'll toss the next distraction."

Lyons keyed his hand radio twice. Blancanales threw the rat to the far side of the other building's roof. The dogs broke into another fury of barking. Paws scratched on tar as they ran to investigate the bait, snarling and yelping. When they found it, the noise got nastier.

"What the hell did you throw?" Lyons asked.

"A dead rat. The dogs are fighting with each other to rip it up. Now's the time. . . ."

The footsteps ran up the stairs. The door opened. Lyons and Blancanales thumbed back the hammers of their autopistols, then eased up.

In the light from the open door, they saw a bearded middle-aged man rush at the dogs. An Uzi hung from his shoulder. Lyons and Blancanales braced their pistols on the wall to sight on the bearded sentry's chest.

"Wait till he's in there with the dogs. . ." Blancanales whispered to Lyons.

The sentry waved a flashlight at the dogs, started kicking them. Dogs yelped, ran away whining. The flashlight found a ragged scrap of rat. The sentry poked at it with his foot.

"Sighting in. . ." Lyons hissed. "Hit him!"

Slugs zipped through the air, a 9mm slug slapping the sentry's jacket, a .45 ACP hollowpoint slamming him back into the crisscrossed barbed wire behind him. Two more slugs bounced him off the wire. He fell flat on the black asphalt, did not move as the dogs ran circles around him, sniffing at the blood.

Lyons spoke into his radio. "Wizard! You through that gate?"

"It's open. What about the dogs?"

"We'll do it." Lyons turned to Blancanales. "Gate's open, but first we waste those dogs. There's no other way. We have to do it. Survival of whoever's fittest to take the grief."

Methodically, Blancanales executed the dogs, his underpowered 9mm subsonic slugs striking with less sound than a slap. Lyons watched over the phosphor dots of his Colt's sights. What he saw was more cruel, somehow, than the killing of men. And more sad. Able Team killed only the bad, and often, sadly, the bad were dumb.

"Goddamn it," Blancanales cursed. He jammed a new mag into the Beretta.

"Forget it, just forget it," Lyons whispered to him, knowing what his friend felt. "We had to. They were in the wrong place at the wrong time. It was them or us. Now let's move it."

As the three men dashed for the gate, other men sprinted up the stairs to the roof. Flashlight beams swept the rooftop and the barbed wire, catching the two Americans and the Egyptian.

Kalashnikov fire ripped the night.

9

STEPPING THROUGH THE GATE in the barbed-wire barrier, Gadgets heard boots hammer the stairs. As he raised his radio to warn his partners, autofire shattered the silence. He fell flat on the roof and slipped out his Beretta.

Gunmen ran across the roof firing Kalashnikovs and Uzis. Gadgets saw the shadowy forms of his partners disappear behind the cover of the brick walls. The gunmen advanced, firing continuously, slugs sparking with the brick, chips of bricks and mortar flying. The barbed-wire fence jerked and swayed as bullets hit the wire, splintered the supports. Gadgets crawled to the cover of a roof fan. He leveled the Beretta.

Shouts in Arabic stopped the rifle fire. A gunman looked over the low wall dividing the roofs of the two apartment buildings. His head jerked back as a silent .45-caliber slug smashed through his face, his skull exploding as bursts of slugs pierced the darkness.

A gunman set down his Uzi and dug into the thigh pocket of his military-style pants. Over the night-glowing sights of his silenced autopistol, Gadgets watched the gunman's silhouette make the motion of pulling a grenade's safety pin. The silhouette stepped forward, an arm arcing back for the throw.

Three 9mm steel-cored slugs ripped through his

shoulder and head. The dying man dropped the grenade as he staggered backward and collapsed. The Muslim terrorists turned to their fallen comrade. One man shouted to the others. Their weapons went silent for an instant as the gunmen dived away.

Thousands of steel fragments shredded them in mid-motion. A pause followed the blast, then the moans and cries began. Gadgets crept backward, retreating from the rooftop.

Lyons and Blancanales leaped through the gate, called out, "Wizard!"

"Where are you?"

"Here!"

"Move it!" Lyons rushed past him, the modified Colt Government Model held out at arm's length, firing round after round as he found targets in the tangle of wounded terrorists.

"Hey!" Gadgets shouted. "Time to get out of here."

Then Blancanales ran past, his Beretta showering brass on Gadgets. Taximan Mohammed followed, Uzi in hand, the bag of thirty-round magazines swinging on his right arm.

Gadgets saw Lyons change Colt mags, snap a shot into the head of a wounded man, take the man's Uzi. Then he was firing bursts down the stairs.

Gadgets ran to join his partners.

At the head of the stairway, Lyons emptied the Uzi into the terrorists on the landing below. Dropping the empty magazine, he returned to the dead gunmen sprawled on the roof to find another loaded Uzi, then another. Blancanales grabbed a bloody AK, snapped shots down the stairs.

"There's no ammunition," Lyons shouted to

Blancanales. "We surprised them; so they grabbed their rifles and ran up here. Check the sentries. . . ."

Ripping open the pockets of one man, Blancanales found a grenade. He flipped over other corpses and found a belt pouch with two Uzi mags.

"Sixty rounds, plus whatever's in the guns. And this. . . ." He held up the grenade.

A gunman lurched up, lashing at Blancanales with a knife. Lyons pointed the Uzi at the wounded man. Blancanales kicked the terrorist in the gut, doubling him over, then kicked him in the back of the head. The man arced back in wide-eyed agony. Blancanales grabbed the knife, stomped down on the terrorist's throat twice. Blood frothed.

"Ready to go?" Blancanales asked, slipping the knife under his belt. He hooked a finger through the safety pin ring of the grenade.

Lyons nodded. Mohammed and Gadgets ran up, Mohammed snatching a glance downstairs. He snapped off a burst. A death-scream ripped the night.

"There's one for Maha'alot," they heard the "Egyptian" say, his expression grim, out of character for the comic taxi driver he claimed to be. Then his manic grin returned. "Let's go, cowboys. Corral full of snakes down there."

Jerking the pin out of the grenade, Blancanales let the lever fly free and threw the frag down the stairway. The heavy thud puffed dust.

Lyons and Blancanales disappeared into the swirling cloud, their feet quick but silent on the blood-splashed stairs. Gadgets braced his Beretta against a railing as he watched for targets. Mohammed waited a second, then crept down the stairs.

The stairs opened to a hallway. Blancanales glanced in one direction, snatched his head back as slugs shrieked past. Lyons searched the several corpses at the foot of the stairs, looped the sling of a second Uzi over his left shoulder, pocketed several Uzi magazines. He snapped out a loaded banana mag for an AK and tossed it to Blancanales.

Pointing in the direction of the autofire, Blancanales shouted, "I'll draw fire, you hit them."

"Forget that! I'll get Muslim volunteers."

"What?"

"Mo-man, help me here!"

With the help of the taxi driver, he lifted a dead terrorist upright and heaved the standing corpse forward.

Autofire from both ends of the hall ripped past the body, one jerking an arm, another spraying gore from its chest. Squatting low, Blancanales sighted on a scarf-wrapped head and punched a 7.62mm hole through the woman's head. She flew back, still alive, her hands clutching at the wound in her skull. Hands grabbed her to drag her out of the line of fire. Blancanales waited until the man exposed a shoulder, then put a slug through his body. The man rolled into the open, and a second slug smashed through his head.

Lyons lay on the floor, squinting through the Uzi's peep-sight, watching a doorway. He saw an exposed arm. He waited. An AK muzzle appeared, then eyes looking for a target. Lyons flicked the trigger, two 9mm rounds pocking the man's forehead. Brains splashed plaster, a rifle held in a dead hand clattered on the hallway tiles.

"Mo-man," Lyons called out. "Another volunteer!"

The "Egyptian" struggled with the deadweight of a second bloody corpse, finally dropping it. "This one crawls...." He shoved the corpse over the smooth tiles with his foot.

Blancanales and Lyons watched both ends of the hall. No terrorists showed themselves.

An arm appeared from a doorway, Lyons fired, but....

"Grenade!" Lyons screamed.

Blancanales and Mohammed ducked down. Lyons saw the olive-drab cylinder hit the tiles, bounce down the stairway alcove. He ducked, cupped his hands over his ears.

Plaster fell from the ceiling and walls, dust clouded up the stairwell. Lyons dashed for the door from where the grenade had come, screaming like a dying man, an Uzi in each hand.

A teenage girl, a mad smile on her face, looked into his eyes, took bursts in the face and chest as Lyons rushed her. He kicked the dying girl aside, sprayed fire into another terrorist behind her.

Lyons surveyed the room. Nothing moved. Stacks of heavy crates lined the walls; words stenciled in Russian and Arabic identified the contents. He saw a curtained closet, glanced under the curtains, saw sandaled feet. He fired a burst. An old man fell out, screaming, holding a gut wound. Lyons fired once into the mullah's head.

Firing continued in the hallway. Lyons let the Uzi hang by its strap to key his hand radio. "This room's clear. Can you break out?"

"We got two rifles at the other end, we'd risk—"

"Don't. I'll try something."

"What?"

"I'll tell you when I know."

Throwing back the lids of the shipping crates, Lyons found Kalashnikov rifles in one case, hundreds of AK magazines in another, then a crate of RPG rockets and launchers. Wasting precious seconds, he continued searching, hoping to find some of the SAM-7 missiles responsible for downing the Air Force jet.

He found no antiaircraft missiles. He reopened the crate of RPGs, loaded a launcher. He went to the corpses and checked their pockets. He buzzed his partners. "I got two frags. I'll bounce them past you. Make your move after the second one, I'll cover—"

"Do it!" Gadgets shouted the length of the hall. "Stop talking! We got to get out of here!"

A grenade bounced past Gadgets, continued to the end of the hall. Covering his ears, Gadgets crouched down beside Mohammed. The blast ricocheted tiny bits of steel off the ceiling and walls and floor. The rifle fire started up again.

The three men sprinted through the dust and smoke. Gadgets saw Lyons crouching outside a door. Did he have a rifle or what?

Sliding on the tiles, jarring into Lyons, Gadgets took cover inside, reached back to grab Mo-man, then Blancanales. The AKs down the hall fired wild.

A shrieking flame answered.

The gift from the Soviet Union rocked the building, but now, instead of murdering Israeli children or housewives, the warhead vaporized the group of fanatics cowering behind a two-foot-thick brick wall.

"Superior firepower," Lyons shouted as he reloaded and recocked the Russian weapon. "Taxi driver. Read what's on those boxes. Any of those SAM-7s?"

"No antiaircraft missiles," Mohammed told them. "Only infantry weapons."

"Rockets for everyone," Lyons ordered. "Get with it! We got to search this hellhole. Room by room."

In the crates, they found vests that served as load-bearing equipment for carrying rockets. The vests looked like bibs with long pockets in the front. The four men slipped into the vests, crammed rockets in the huge pockets. Gadgets and Mohammed took launchers. They went to the door.

Gadgets turned to Blancanales and Lyons. "What happens if we fire these point-blank?"

"Don't know. . . ."

"Don't!" Mohammed told them. "A friend did in Lebanon."

"Move it," Lyons said. "Find those SAM-7s and we go home."

Stepping to the doorway, Mohammed stayed behind the shelter of the wall and fired diagonally across the hall. Backblast seared the apartment's wall. The blast itself sent chunks of brick bouncing through the hallway.

Gadgets went next, leaning into the hallway, firing at the back apartment. Heavy with weapons and rockets, they rushed into the swirling dust and smoke. Pausing only to check on the position of their partners, Gadgets and Mohammed fired rockets continually, reloading on the run.

Vast holes appeared in apartment walls. Rushing through doorways, they looked for more of the Russian-marked crates. They found none. The other rooms held only personal possessions of the terrorist group. They saw walls covered with posters of Khomeini and Arafat and the red, white, green and black flag of the PLO.

Flames licked from burning furnishings. Through the smoke, Mohammed saw a movement in a doorway. He ran to the door, shoved the launcher out at arm's length and fired blind. The explosion in the apartment threw Blancanales back against the wall.

Slugs punched the wall next to Blancanales's head. Lyons spotted a form in the smoke, fired an Uzi in each hand.

"Down!" Gadgets shouted out. "Rocket ready!"

The others went flat as Gadgets dodged from a doorway and fired the RPG from his hip.

The rocket's explosion sheared away a wall, smashed out a back wall.

Blancanales crawled forward to glance into the last apartment. He saw only a torso and legs remaining of the gunman. Scanning the apartment quickly, he spotted no shipping crates.

"No rockets in there. Maybe the old man meant the RPGs."

"Ironman," Gadgets called over to him. "Time to get out of here! The Egyptians will call out the army!"

"Not yet. We'll search the other rooms on the floor, get out over the roofs."

"Those rockets! Look!" Mohammed shouted. He stood at a hole in the wall, gazing down at the alley behind the apartment building.

Evening air cooled their faces as they all looked down. They saw teenagers scrambling over a truck. Some of the young men waved AK rifles at onlookers to warn them back, others struggled to cover the rack of rocket tubes on the back of the truck with a black tarp.

"Dig that," Mohammed laughed. "A Katyusha. That's what that mullah saw...."

The truck carried a rack of forty 122mm rocket-launching tubes. Though capable of raining a salvo of high explosives on a target, the rockets of a "Stalin's Organ" flew like artillery shells, without infrared or radar-homing warheads. A Katyusha presented no threat to high-flying aircraft.

"Wrong rockets, wrong goddamn place," Lyons cursed.

"As long as we're here anyway...." Gadgets pulled off the safety cap of an RPG, cocked the launcher's hammer. "Stand back for backblast!"

Leaning through the shattered bricks, Gadgets sighted on the rack of rocket tubes and pulled the trigger. The flash lighted the night. "Katyusha out of order!" Mangled terrorists flew from the flaming truck. Bystanders scattered, though Gadgets had known his aim was sure enough to avoid reckless endangerment.

A blast threw them back. Shock rocked the floor and walls. Sections of ceiling fell. As Blancanales hit the heaving floor, he saw the rear wall of the apartment building fall away. A wave of flame rushed upward. The night returned for an instant, then another sheet of flame roared up.

Gadgets lay on the floor, stunned. Blancanales

grabbed him by the coat sleeve to drag him back.

"Secondaries! This is not the place to be!"

Mohammed took Gadgets's other arm. Lyons rose to his feet. He staggered with an Uzi in his right hand and another Uzi dangling by a strap from his left wrist.

"Come on! The building's falling!" Blancanales shoved Lyons over to Mohammed the taximan. "Move him out of here."

"Hey, it's been a blast. But we gotta go!"

Another explosion brought down more plaster and bricks. A slab of plaster broke over Lyons's shoulders. He shrugged off the white dust, staggered after the others, steadying himself with his left hand against the wall. Blood streamed from his hair, flowed down his face. Mohammed glanced back at him, grabbed his arm and helped him toward the stairs.

"You all right, man? You ready to go up those stairs?"

"The rockets are here," Lyons gasped, the Uzi clattering against the wall. "They're here someplace."

"We got their rockets! So forget about finding any more, okay? Please? We hit any more rockets in this place, we check in El Motel Allah."

"I mean, in Cairo. In Cairo. The rockets are in Cairo." He staggered, blew blood off his lip. "Somewhere."

10

THROUGH THE THICK bullet-resistant glass of the limousine window, tinted gray to block out the desert glare and the gaze of the common people, the lights became abstract patterns of amber and pale blue. Katz watched the distorted images of the Cairo night float past as he listened to Sadek and Parks.

The young CIA officer, his face unshaven and lined, eyes red with fatigue, talked quietly with the bored, always-dapper Sadek. They reviewed notes, cross-checking names and addresses against a map of the greater Cairo area.

"I understand the restraints on your personnel, but we must have information on the government employees at the airport."

"It will take weeks," Sadek repeated. "We do not investigate individuals simply because they express sympathy for these groups or their ideals. We respect religious expression."

"Religious expression? Mobs screaming 'Death to the Great Satan'? Let's start with the workers from the international airport that my people recognized."

"Often what a foreigner might consider fanaticism is only the expression of a fervent devotion to Allah. However, we are aware of the activities of certain individuals. Next month, we will have a complete list of suspects. . . . ''

That petty, self-important bureaucrat, Katz thought as he observed the Egyptian officer, listened to his smooth excuses. The flashy English and American styles, the LCD watch, perfect tie—all of it offended the Israeli colonel.

Katz had no respect for this playboy. Despite the bureaucrat's record of service with the Egyptian Second Army, Sadek was unlikely to have been a veteran of the Sinai. Perhaps a veteran of office politics, corridor wars, but not of fighting in the dust and diesel-filth and horror of an armored assault.

Sadek: wealthy, pompous, useless. He had no doubt purchased a military commission, then bribed his way to a career. Such men crowded the government and armed forces. They had led the army to constant defeat.

Sadek once accepted the gold of the Soviets, now he took the dollars of the Americans. A loyal and trustworthy friend to whatever foreign power dominated Egypt: Turkish, English, Soviet, American.

And Parks thought of Sadek as a patriot. The Americans bought the mediocre government leaders, the vainglorious army officers of many nations— Egypt; El Salvador; years before, Vietnam—and called them patriots.

A purchased friend of the United States. Katz had no reason to trust Sadek. The fanatics of the Muslim Brotherhood had infiltrated every branch of the Egyptian armed forces and government. Why not also the corrupt?

The limousine's radio phone buzzed.

"Parks here...." He listened for a moment, then passed the phone to Sadek. After a moment, Sadek slammed down the phone.

"Terrorism. A major incident this time."

PARKS AND KATZ had not waited to investigate the fanatics. Minutes after the SAM-7 missiles had destroyed the secret U-2, the surveillance of the airport personnel had become the focus of an ongoing program.

After the disaster of the Iranian Revolution, the CIA had assembled a group of researchers and investigators to monitor the activities of the Muslim extremists in Egypt and Libya. This secret group operated independent of the Egyptian intelligence services. Sadek knew nothing of it.

Eighteen months earlier, the American force of investigators had discovered the plot to murder President Sadat. But when the CIA had notified the Egyptians, the warning had never reached the officers responsible for President Sadat's security. The next day, as Sadat had saluted a military parade, Muslim fanatics had jumped from a truck and had assaulted the reviewing stand where their president stood, firing their Soviet-supplied Kalashnikov automatic rifles point-blank into the only Arab who had had the courage to make both war and peace with the Israelis.

Since that day, the CIA had maintained a careful distance from all Egyptian security officers.

Within minutes of learning of the missile-downed American spy plane, the task force had assembled files of names and photographs of known fanatics employed at the international airport by the government of Egypt and the hundreds of private companies. Parks and Katz had then organized the operation against the fanatics. Parks had wanted to include Sadek in the mission planning. Katz had forbidden Parks to reveal any detail of the operation to any Egyptian.

Now, as their limousine sped into one of the quarters of the ancient city, Sadek briefing Parks on the future Egyptian investigation, an unmarked United States Air Force F-16 taxied onto the runway of Cairo International Airport.

"Executive Underwriters' shuttle jet, requesting permission for takeoff...."

ALMOST A MILE AWAY, the late-night shift of flight controllers glanced at radar screens empty of tourist flights. Talking and joking as they chain-smoked, they followed the course of an air-freight flight crossing the Mediterranean coast. As he gulped coffee, one of the men watched a controller monitoring an outgoing flight at a console.

"Please wait for updated atmospheric data," Aziz Shawan murmured into his headset's microphone. The controller reached to the tiny pager at his belt, pressed the unit three times.

Seated a few feet away, the other controller noted the action. He excused himself from his friends and left the tower's flight-control center.

He went to the lounge. In a few hurried steps, he checked the restroom's toilet stalls for other employees, then returned to the lounge. He dropped a coin into the pay phone.

What he had seen, and this call to the Egyptian

secret police, would earn a new color television for his home.

But the number he dialed rang an office in the American aircraft hangar at the far end of the airport complex.

In fluent, idiomatic Arabic, a CIA agent took the information. Slamming down the phone, he pressed an intercom button. "Our turkey in the con-tower called. He saw Aziz Shawan dispatch our flight, then press his pager, but not in response to any signal from the pager."

"Three tones, right?"

"Yeah. You got it?"

"Confirmed. Our team is listening into the transmission now. Evidently the Muslims are alerting their headquarters."

On the runway, the pilot of the F-16 eased forward the throttle. As he gained speed, the runway lights became parallel streaks of light. Then the interceptor hurtled into the night. Holding down his speed, the pilot followed the flight path of the U-2 destroyed two nights before.

Watching the display of the downward-looking radar, the pilot waited for the blips of uprushing missiles. One gloved hand reached for the switch of the electronic counter-measures. He spoke into his helmet's microphone. "This is the Roadrunner. All set to smoke the Coyote."

Below, in the streets of Cairo, agents waited in cars and trucks. Technicians listened as the Muslim Brotherhood agent at the international airport told his superior about the American Air Force jet. In seconds, signals went out to the missile units.

"These crazies are organized!" one technician told another. "Flight controller to SAM launchers, ninety seconds."

"And ten more for launch! There go the missiles!" The agent spoke into his radio. "We saw a launch from a truck. The truck's moving. We're following...."

In the cockpit of the F-16, the pilot saw the green points of the SAM-7 missiles appear on his display screen. He flicked the electronic-counter-measures switch, pulled back on the throttle. Giving the engines full power, the pilot took his jet far away from the threat of the Soviet missiles.

Laughing to himself, the pilot thought of a cartoon roadrunner streaking an acetate desert, leaving the hungry coyote behind in a cloud of dust.

"Beep, beep."

ZAKI PULLED DOWN the rolling door of the garage. Bloody and dirty, Able Team staggered from the taxis. Lyons lurched to one of the Fiats and sprawled on the hood, using it as a lounge. Blood caked his hair to his skull.

Examining the wound with a calm, experienced eye, Abdul poured water on Lyons's hair, sponged away the gore. "Open your eyes for a moment, sir. Look at the light. Good, good. Do you have any pain? Are you dizzy? We have doctors available if—"

"You got some food available?" Lyons interrupted. "My head's okay, but my stomach's killing me."

"Yes, sir. I'll see exactly what was provided. Would you like a folding cot? Colonel Katzenelenbogen anticipated your comforts, also."

"Just so I don't have to lie down on the concrete...."

Blancanales surveyed the interior of windowless garage. He glanced from the shadowed corners to the few boxes stacked against one wall. He saw no exit other than the steel roll-down door. "Where are the prisoners?"

"They were taken for interrogation," Abdul answered.

"By who?" Lyons demanded.

The three taxi drivers looked to one another. Abdul continued, "I'm quite sure the embassy will receive transcripts of all the information."

"The old man needed immediate hospital care," Zaki reminded them.

"Hey!" Lyons shouted. "You're not hearing me. I asked you who's got them?"

Mo-man laughed. "Well, hey yourself, bad man. Why do you want them? Target practice? Ain't you killed enough of them tonight?"

Blancanales went to Lyons. "Let it go. You know who's got them. The local Mossad franchise."

"Maybe," Mohammed admitted.

"Then why don't you say so?" barked Lyons.

"It's called the 'option to deny,'" Blancanales said.

"Political double-talk is what it's called," Lyons muttered.

Abdul checked the boxes. He returned with a folding aluminum cot, and he set it out for Lyons. "Here, sir. And we have blankets if you would like to sleep."

Gadgets was searching through the boxes. He

called out, "Dig this! They got hot food in here. Look at this."

"What is it?" Blancanales asked, walking across the garage. "What's that I smell?"

Gadgets opened a flat Styrofoam carton. "Steak! It's hot. All right, man! Someone out there loves us. Ironman, forget about the rockets for ten minutes. Get a steak. Take a break."

The three men of Able Team and their "Egyptian" helpers crowded around the cartons, finding Styrofoam boxes of steak dinners, containers of hot coffee and chocolate. Other boxes contained more folding cots, blankets, loaded Uzi mags and .45-caliber ammunition. Gadgets crammed a handful of french fries in his mouth, gulped. "Whoever they are, they know what we need."

Lyons glanced at his watch. "I want to clean up and be ready to move again in an hour."

"What the hell," Gadgets said. "We don't even know where we're *going* next."

"Okay, Mossad Man," Lyons addressed Mohammed the taxi driver. "You seem to know everything. Tell us where we're going next. Where are those rockets?"

Mohammed set down his Styrofoam plate. Making his face the solemn mask of a fortune-teller, he brushed his hands over wavy hair, ratting it to an electric tangle. He rolled his eyes, raised his hands to the soot-blackened ceiling of the garage. "I see...I see...."

Despite himself, Lyons laughed, the tension and exhaustion gone for the instant of the jive-talking young man's routine. Mohammed bugged his eyes, fixed Lyons in a stare, his face frozen in comic terror. He shook his head, blinked his eyes. "Jeeeeezus."

"What?" Lyons demanded. "Tell me."

"What I saw? I looked into your heart and, man, I'm sure glad you ain't after me. That Muslim Brotherhood better say its prayers, 'cause there's a heart of darkness abroad tonight!"

WHITE-UNIFORMED POLICE OFFICERS with flashlights guided the limousine through the squad cars and the fire engines. An ambulance turned from an alley and accelerated away, its siren shrieking. Smoke drifted from the alley mouth, evening wind dissipating the acrid haze through the neighborhood. Sadek knocked on the Plexiglas partition. "Here, driver. Thank you."

Sadek stepped out, held the door open for Katz and Parks. In the alley, they saw the floodlights of emergency vehicles. Shadowy forms moved in the glowing haze. Firemen directed streams of water onto the smoking hulk of truck.

A plainclothes security man, his Kalashnikov slung over his back, hurried to Sadek, saluted. They spoke quickly, the security man shaking his head, pointing to the street.

"He says there are hazards in the alley. We must enter through the front."

They hurried around the corner, passed restaurants with tables covered with abandoned meals, coffee shops littered with fallen plaster and broken cups. Shopkeepers pulled steel grates across their shattered windows.

Sadek briefed his American associates. "Twenty

or more dead. Witnesses tell of a gunfight, then many explosions. Finally, the great explosion in the alley. My officers reported finding extremist literature in the rooms.''

''Muslim Brotherhood?'' Katz asked.

''No. Palestinian. My country offers refuge to brother Arabs. Sometimes our brothers abuse our trust.''

Paramilitary officers in fatigues and helmets stood aside as Sadek led his associates up the stairs. The younger Sadek and Parks took the stairs two at a time, leaving the limping Katz behind. He glanced ahead, saw another paramilitary trooper, a barrel-chested officer in a beret, stop Sadek and Parks.

Speaking with Sadek, the officer swept his eyes up and down Parks, then Katz as he limped to the landing. Katz saw the officer's lip arch with a sneer. Then the young man saluted Sadek and paced away.

''He told me they have not yet removed or even covered the bodies,'' said Sadek. ''It is not a sight for weak stomachs, he told me.''

''I've seen everything.'' Parks dismissed the words with a casual wave of his hand. ''And I'm sure Mr. Steiner has seen more.''

Parks ran up the next flight of stairs, slipped and fell in coagulated blood. He jumped back, gasping.

Debris that had been a human body littered the stairs. A blast had sprayed the wall with blood, left the pearl-pink of shattered skull on the old tile steps. Parks turned his face away, continued carefully up the stairs, passing a white-smocked orderly in elbow-high plastic gloves. Katz and Sadek followed Parks.

Soldiers and investigators moved through the ruins

of the apartment building's third floor. Orderlies laid bodies on plastic-sheeted stretchers. Two young men argued over an arm, one orderly pointing to a mangled corpse on a stretcher, the other shaking his head. They resolved the argument by putting the arm in approximate position on the gory corpse, found it did not match, and slung it into a bag.

Walking through the hall, Katz glanced into a room. He saw a poster of Khomeini. He picked up a pamphlet, leafed through it. The writer preached annihilation of Christians, Jews, deviate Muslims—but only the men and male children; the women and girls would be used for the pleasure of the warriors. Yakov Katzenelenbogen threw the literature to the floor in disgust; Phoenix Force's senior member was to a degree hardened against bloodshed, but he found sick ideas forever repugnant.

Katz followed a few steps behind Sadek, watching the well-groomed and modishly dressed officer step over blood and gore to avoid staining his English wing tips.

Sadek spoke with a soldier, then turned to Katz. "There was fighting on the roof. We should go there."

Following the bloody stairs into the smoke-hazed midnight, they coughed as the slight wind blew drifts of soot and smoke past them.

"Where is Mr. Parks?" Sadek asked.

Katz glanced back down the stairs. "I don't know."

"Perhaps his stomach. . . ."

They smiled at their friend's discomfort. Katz never took his attention from the Egyptian. He stayed at Sadek's side, watching him, noting the small details the man noted. He saw Sadek wave a flashlight over dead dogs, then several corpses. The flashlight's beam held on wounds. A few steps farther, Sadek found brass casings.

Taking an envelope from his jacket pocket, he scooped up two 9mm casings. He found a .45-caliber casing, picked it up with the point of a pen, studied it for a moment. Then that shell went into the envelope.

"Steiner! Steiner!" A voice called out. Returning to the stairs, Katz saw Parks waving him down.

As Katz limped down to the landing, Parks blurted out, "We're in motion at the airport, sir! We got an investigation. It's a whole new ball game."

Nodding, Katz glanced around them, saw three Egyptians within earshot. At the head of the stairs, he heard Sadek speaking in Arabic with a plainclothes officer. Katz heard Sadek instruct the officer to "...take the shell casings to the laboratory."

Katz pointed to the silver rod of an antenna that stuck out of the coat pocket of Parks's suit.

"Your driver radioed the message?"

"Yes, just this minute. My men are following a suspect...."

"Is that radio scrambler-equipped?"

"This?" Parks held up the radio. He looked at the switches, turned the radio in his hand as if looking for printed specifications. "I don't know...."

11

BREAKING DOWN the modified Colt Government Model, Lyons examined it for damage or unusual wear. He released the magazine and thumbed out the cartridges. He checked for grit or lint on the ramp or feed lips and laid the magazines on the clean canvas of his folding cot. A tiny wrench removed the set screw from the suppressor, allowing the oval cylinder to unscrew from the threaded barrel. He put the suppressor in one of the empty coffee containers, filled the container with solvent and left the suppressor to soak.

He depressed the disassembly latch that replaced the Colt's slide stop. The pistol's slide and barrel assembly slipped forward and apart like a Beretta. The short high-tension recoil spring shot into his palm.

Lyons noted that Gadgets was watching. "Seen my new Colt?"

"Konzaki made that? How can you put a silencer on the barrel of a 1911? The barrel flops up and down during the cycle...."

"Look." Lyons held up the slide assembly. He moved the barrel. "See? It's different. And the ejector. And the interlink between the barrel and the slide. Andrzej says the barrel doesn't unlock as

Browning designed it. It's like a Beretta now. When you fire, the barrel and slide travel back, the barrel unlocks for an instant but stays straight, the slide continues back and the brass ejects. That's why the ejection port is cut all the way across. The brass flies straight up. The barrel stays straight on line the whole cycle. And there are big changes in the sear mechanism.''

Studying the modified components, the internal parts still bearing machining marks, here and there the heat marks of micro-welds, Gadgets joked, "Colt Frankenstein!''

"Decent accuracy, fires silent bursts of full-velocity hollowpoints. You saw what I did with it. I got no complaints about how it looks.''

Gadgets squatted down, balanced on the balls of his feet. He glanced to their taxi drivers, spoke too quietly for the others to hear. "Yeah, I saw what you did tonight. I got to talk to you. . . .''

"This a criticism session?''

"Nah, man. You were beautiful tonight. For a guy who ain't even a vet, you do real well. Wish you'd been with me in Nam.''

"When we got the surprise on that roof, you yelled for us to get out of there. You wanted to retreat.''

"Well. . . yeah. That would've been the intelligent thing to do.'' Gadgets called out, "Politician! Over here. Help me with some wording. . . . Dig it, Carl. Don't get defensive. I'm trying to talk philosophy with you.''

"I wanted those rockets. I didn't know they weren't the right kind of rockets. That old man steered us wrong.''

"No problem with that. It's cool. They could've had a million SAM-7s. Like you said, we could have gone home tonight. Rosario, our pal thinks I'm criticizing him when I say it would have been intelligent to have retreated tonight...."

Blancanales nodded. He pulled up another cot, sat down. "Could have gone wrong."

"It did go wrong," Lyons told them. He dipped a bore brush in the coffee container of solvent and began to swab out the Colt's short barrel. "We didn't get the missiles."

"See? He thinks I'm criticizing him," said Gadgets. "Hey, I want to introduce the concept of an 'Honorable Withdrawal.' To retreat from an unfavorable turn of circumstancce is not a crime. Dig who's telling you this. Old Gadgets Schwarz, Special Forces, retired. Now active in Very Special Forces."

"That's why I'm glad I'm with you," Blancanales said. "I figure I learn something once in a while."

"I think you're trying to prove something, you know that?" smiled Gadgets.

"I *am* trying to prove something," Lyons insisted. His voice had risen. He caught himself, lowered his tone to an urgent whisper. "I'm trying to prove I can make a difference. And for the last year or so, I have. I've helped my country, I've helped my people. I've helped people I didn't know existed...."

"Okay, okay," Gadgets grinned. "But just understand—next time we're outnumbered, outgunned, ambushed and naked in the kill zone, retreat *is* an option."

The buzz of Gadgets's relay radio unit sounded.

Blancanales went to the hood of a taxi, brought the radio to where Gadgets knelt with Lyons.

Gadgets put the handset to his ear and listened. He looked to Lyons and Blancanales.

"The rockets. . . ."

As HIS TAXI CRUISED through streets lurid with neon Arabic signs, Gadgets received a call from Katz via scrambler-encoded radio. "I separated from the embassy group. This will be my only opportunity to brief you. Please take notes so that you may brief your compatriots."

"How about a four-way?" Gadgets suggested. "A conference call. If you don't mind the drivers hearing. . . ."

"Where are the others?"

"In the cabs."

"Very well."

Keying his hand radio, Gadgets buzzed the others. "Politician. Ironman. Conference with the diplomat."

"Waiting," Blancanales answered.

"So what's going on?" Lyons asked.

"Gentlemen. I do not have much time to speak. Soon I must rejoin our Agency associates. First, I inspected the site of your action. That group is now inoperative. Second, I received a report from friends who questioned your prisoners. You neutralized a group of Muslim Brotherhood and PLO assassins. That group planned a series of strikes against American and Western European diplomats. The attack on the limousines leaving the embassy was the first of the series. Our friends determined that the group did not participate in the attack on the jet.''

"Yeah," Lyons interrupted. "We found out. They had rockets but not SAMs. All that for nothing.''

"Your time was not wasted," Katz told him. "And simultaneous with your action, the Agency scored something of a success of its own. An hour ago, another secret flight left the airport.''

"Was it hit?" Blancanales asked.

"No. This time, it was an F-16 with electronic counter-measures and the speed to escape the missiles—''

"They get a fix on the ragheads?" Lyons broke in again.

"That was the purpose of the flight. I assure you, the Air Force is not risking the lives of pilots for nothing, not at a time when your American flyers in Egypt are calling all of their planes lead-lined coffins. The Agency had several teams of technicians in place and waiting. The technicians monitored a signal from the airport alerting the main terrorist group in the city. Then another team in the city monitored communications between the group's command center and several units dispersed throughout the greater Cairo area.''

"These crazies sound organized," Gadgets said. "They got good equipment?''

"They don't have encoding. But the technicians say the radios are first-quality commercial equipment. Although the technicians could not pinpoint the headquarters, they did get to the approximate area of a unit as they launched a missile.

"The terrorists launched the missile from a truck.

The technicians followed the truck to a warehouse. Agency teams now have it under surveillance.

"It is possible that warehouse is the headquarters of the terrorist commander.

"However, our esteemed associates in the Agency may have compromised the operation. While we examined the site of your action against the Muslim and PLO terrorists, the driver of our limousine relayed the news of the warehouse to the walkie-talkie of Parks. I examined the radio. It is not equipped with encoding. It is possible the opposition also received the information."

"Those short hairs are going to walk into another ambush for sure," said Gadgets.

"Gentlemen," intoned the voice of Katz, "it will be another hour before Parks and his men move on the warehouse. Is it possible for you to resolve the problem before that time?"

"You want us to volunteer to check out the kill zone?" Lyons demanded. "Is that what you're asking?"

"Exactly."

12

"COMMANDER OMAR!" a warrior called out. "Americans!"

The elegant leader of the National Front's group in Cairo descended the wooden steps from the offices. He saw his Islamic soldiers clutching their Soviet autorifles and rocket launchers. They lusted for battle.

Only thirty minutes before, Omar had danced with a beautiful French girl at a reception for the PLO. But a signal from his beeper had taken him away from the champagne and Brazilian jazz rhythms. Rushing to this warehouse-fortress within the city, he learned of the escape of the American spy plane. Then his Libyan electronics technician told him of the snatches of radio messages between the CIA officers.

Thank Allah, thought the commander, *that the United States had such greed it would sell the marvels of modern electronics to its enemies!* Though his technician had learned his skills in the Soviet schools of South Yemen, he had worked with American components to monitor and record the communications of the Americans. Now, armed with foreknowledge of the Central Intelligence Agency plot, Omar and his warriors could slash out and kill, then escape untouched. Omar smiled to his warriors.

"I know. I have known of their plot all this night. And I am ready. Tonight, we kill many Americans."

HEADLIGHTS SWEPT THE WALLS. As Abdul stopped the taxi, Lyons stepped into the garbage of the gutter. The air stank of rot and insecticide. During the day, farm trucks and vendors jammed the street, shoppers crowding around tailgates and merchants' stalls to buy foods fresh from the farms of the Nile. Now, where thousands walked in the daylight, Lyons walked alone. The gray luminescence of the Cairo night left the street market in darkness. No lights showed in the windows and doorways of the warehouses opening to the market.

Lyons moved through shadows, found the steel ladder that the cab's headlights had revealed. He flicked on his penlight to see steel sheet and padlock barring unauthorized entry.

"We need a tire iron," he whispered into his hand radio.

"On our way," Blancanales answered.

Far down the block, another set of headlights flashed in the darkness. Rolling to a stop behind Abdul, Blancanales and Zaki left their cab. Zaki opened the trunk, took out a tire iron and an airline flight bag. Lyons blinked his penlight to reveal where he waited.

By the glow of the penlight, Zaki shoved the point of the tire iron through the shackle. Snapping the padlock away, they swung the steel gate aside.

Wordlessly, Lyons went first, the rusted steel of the ladder creaking with his weight. His hands felt the grit of years of dust and soot. As he neared the roof, he slowed, listening for any sounds or voices above him. He heard nothing. Finally, he eased his head over the edge.

He saw only a black expanse of roof and shadows. An army could be hiding in the darkness. He had to chance it. Here, a block away from the warehouse of the Muslim terrorists, he did not expect sentries. Hoping he wouldn't get a surprise, he slipped over the top of the wall.

Crouching in the shadow, he waited, listening, modified Colt in his hand. Somewhere on the roof, a fan flailed steel against steel. He heard the popping of a motorcycle.

He watched for shifts in the rooftop silhouettes of pipes and wires and fan housings. In the distance, a gentle wind carried dust from the desert, blurring the lights of modern Cairo's high-rise towers. After minutes without moving, Lyons keyed his hand radio's transmit button twice, then twice again.

The ladder creaked with steps. Lyons dashed across the roof, flattened himself against a fan housing. He listened for movement or the mechanical click of a released safety. He heard only the sound of a shoe scraping the wall behind him. Lyons snapped his fingers twice to give Blancanales his position.

A crouching Zaki followed seconds later. He unzipped his flight bag and pulled out his Uzi. He shoved extra magazines into the pockets of his jeans, then joined Lyons and Blancanales.

"Wizard," Lyons whispered into his hand radio, "we're on the roof."

"See anyone?"

"No. Stand by, we're moving."

Loud in the early-morning quiet, tarred sheet metal flexed under their shoes as they hurried across the roof. The huge warehouse spanned the block. As they approached the other side, they moved slower, pausing behind ventilator pipes. Then they dashed forward, one man at a time.

Lyons crouched at the low wall and peered down at the street. Directly beneath them, a CIA surveillance van parked with several other trucks. Diagonally across the intersection of two streets, the warehouse of the Muslim terrorist group showed no lights. From their position, Lyons and Blancanales scanned the roof for sentries.

"There," Blancanales pointed.

"Where?"

"The outline of that water tower. There's the silhouette of an arm. A shoulder. See the rifle stock?"

"Yeah. But I don't see any way to get there."

"The Wizard will have to go up on that other block." Lyons pointed to a line of buildings beyond the terrorist warehouse.

"Hey, Americans!" Zaki hissed. "Down there, the sidewalk!"

"What?"

They looked down, saw a section of the concrete sidewalk hinge back. Black forms with pistols crept from the hole.

Lyons keyed his hand radio. "Wizard! We got four ragheads coming up out of the ground. They're moving in on the CIA boys. Where are you?"

"Coming up out of the ground?" Gadgets asked, incredulous.

"They've got a tunnel under the street," Lyons told him. "They're going to take the men in the car...."

"Which car? Which street?"

"Below us. It's the car on the south corner of the hideout."

As Lyons spoke, Blancanales slipped out his silenced Beretta and folded down the left-hand grip. He leaned over the edge, bracing the 9mm autopistol against the wall. He sighted on the shadows three stories beneath them. "Can't get...can't get a line on them. They're under an awning...."

Tempered glass shattered. A man cried out. The dull smashes of other car windows breaking echoed in the early-morning darkness.

"Too late," Blancanales sighed.

"It's over, Wizard. Silenced pistols."

Blancanales jerked his autopistol up again, sighted straight down. "One's alive! They're taking one of the...."

Two of the black-clothed forms dragged an American to the trapdoor. But the terrorists crouched too close to the struggling American.

At the awkward angle from the roof, Blancanales could not fire without hitting the Agency man. Then the gunmen disappeared down the hole with the prisoner.

Lyons knew what the American faced: merciless torture and mutilation. He keyed the transmit again. "Wizard, they took a man alive."

A breathless voice answered. "I'm on the corner, looking at them. Two of them. They're ransacking the car. And that trapdoor's still open. What do you say we get our associate back?"

HIS HANDS AND ANKLES BOUND, the American rolled into a ball on the concrete, trying to protect his face and stomach from the kicks and rifle butts of the attackers. One terrorist slammed a boot into the prisoner's back again and again, finally finding a kidney. The American arched back in agony.

As kicks thudded into the prisoner's gut, one warrior slammed the butt plate of his Soviet AK into the prisoner's face, smashing the nose.

Omar stopped his warriors. "He cannot die before we question him."

The American groaned. Blood bubbled from his broken face. The knot of Arabs gathered around the semiconscious prisoner. They laughed, jeered. Omar stooped and tried to grasp the American's short hair but couldn't. He grabbed the man's ear, instead, jerking his head from the concrete.

"Do you feel pain?" Omar asked in English. "Do you suffer? Wait. Soon you will know all the pain of the world. You will beg for death. Then I will give you more pain."

The elegant Egyptian stood. "Take him to the truck. We leave immediately!"

THE TAXIS ROLLED TO A SILENT STOP. Lyons and Blancanales stepped out and sprinted for the corner. The two warriors searched the shadows of the street for Gadgets, saw him nowhere. Blancanales clicked his hand radio three times.

"Too late, dudes," Gadgets's voice answered. "Had to do it myself."

They looked around the corner, saw Gadgets and Mohammed weave through trucks parked on the sidewalk. Motioning their taxis to follow, Lyons and Blancanales continued to the open trapdoor.

Water trickled in the darkness below the pavement. The stink of sewage and old, old stones drifted up.

Gadgets pointed to the corpse of a gunman sprawled in the gutter. "Look at his legs. Only his shoes are wet."

Lyons glanced up at his partners. "We go in?"

Gadgets nodded.

"No other way," Blancanales agreed.

They went to their taxis. Taking off their sports coats, they slipped on Kevlar-and-steel battle armor. Gadgets and Blancanales filled the front pouches with magazines for their Uzis. Grenades went in the side pockets. Lyons dropped a few grenades in his front pouches, slung a bandolier of Atchisson mags over his armor. All three men wore their silenced autopistols on web belts.

Mohammed ran up. He now wore battle armor and a bandolier heavy with Uzi mags. He offered Lyons a flashlight.

"I got one," Lyons told him.

"Ain't got one like this. This is one of theirs. Look at the glass."

The lens had been tinted blue. "All right. Smart move."

"Just 'cause I talk like an American, don't mean I is stupid."

Snapping back the actuator of his Atchisson, Lyons chambered a 12-gauge round of high-velocity double-ought and number two steel shot and flicked on the safety. He walked to the trapdoor, the weight of his armor and weapons and ammunition making every step a conscious effort.

Gadgets slung two Armburst rocket launchers over his back.

"Rockets?" Lyons asked, looking back.

"Why not?" Gadgets shrugged. "Suppose we can't find our way out...?"

The aluminum ladder swayed as Lyons descended into the Cairo underworld.

13

EVERY BREATH brought pain. Jake Newton flinched against an imagined kick, passed out again as a wave of pain crashed over his consciousness. He floated for a moment in peace, without fear, far away from his body. But he returned.

Forcing himself to consider the pain, he remained motionless, his eyes closed, his breathing slow. He listened. Voices spoke in Arabic. He heard the clank of metal, the sound of footsteps on concrete.

He eased an eye open. Specks of light gleamed through fabric. He lay in the back of a canvas-covered truck. It was not moving. Looking around him, he saw his blood puddling on the wood slats. His hands were tied in front of him. His slacks were filthy and bloody.

Pain ripped through his ribs and back as he tried the knots around his wrists. Then he strained to separate his ankles and felt the ropes binding his feet together.

They had taken him hostage. He remembered sitting in the car, watching the roof line of the warehouse through an infrared scope. Then the car windows burst inward. He never saw the terrorists who beat him. He only remembered the shock of steel smashing down on his skull again and again.

The kicking and beating on the concrete remained only a confusion of pain.

When would the questions begin? Would he survive the interrogation? Considering what the terrorists had already done to him, he could not expect to live through it.

The truck swayed on its springs. Jake lay utterly motionless as boots walked the truckbed. A heavy box dropped. The boots scuffed, hesitated. A boot toe smashed into the back of his head. Despite himself, he gasped.

Laughter rang out. The boots stomped away. He heard the boots drop to the concrete.

Jake waited to the count of one hundred before opening his eyes again. He turned slightly to look behind him. He saw the crates stacked there. But none of the terrorists.

Uprights of stamped sheet metal held up the truck's canvas canopy. Watching the tailgate, Jake reached to the nearest upright and dragged the knots binding his wrists over the sharp edge.

BLUE LIGHT SPARKLED on flowing filth. The tinted flashlight in his left hand, his right gripping the Colt, Lyons followed the narrow walkway through the ancient sewer. Behind him, Gadgets held his silenced Beretta ready. Blancanales and Mohammed followed a few steps behind.

Things scurried in the darkness around them. Small stones fell from the crumbling walls. Ahead of them, they saw only total darkness.

The chill fetid air of the age-old sewer touched their faces like foul hands. Nerves and the exertion of walking with the weight of their armor and weapons forced Able Team to breathe deep the stench. After a minute, the noses went dead. But the thick, poisonous atmosphere tore at their throats, made their senses dull, their thoughts slow.

"Ironman," Gadgets whispered. "Stop. Kill the light."

Lyons flicked off the light and stood motionless in the absolute black. He stared forward, straining his eyes for a light.

"It's been a hundred paces," Blancanales hissed.

Only trickling water and the small noises of scuttling creatures broke the silence. Lyons heard his blood rushing through his arteries, the boom of his heart. Air rasped over the membranes of his throat.

"Zilch," Gadgets admitted.

Waving the light ahead of him, Lyons continued forward. A rush of air swept past him. Lyons turned off his flashlight. Mo-man's light died an instant later.

Clean air washed over his face like clear, cool water. Lyons gulped the delicious breeze as he thumbed his Colt's safety down two clicks to full autoburst. He heard other safeties snap off.

A pale white luminescence glowed from a wall ahead of them. Footsteps and clattering metal echoed. A blue light appeared, whipped about, then bobbed toward them. A second blue light came from the wall.

The white glow backlit four armed men. The first and last men held flashlights. They all carried autorifles.

Lyons eased himself flat. Behind him, a knee cracked. Metal touched stone. Able Team waited.

A voice spoke in Arabic; a man laughed. A third voice hissed the others quiet. Able Team waited until the blue light of the pointman revealed Lyons flat on his belly, the oval cylinder of the silenced Colt pointing up.

Silent .45 slugs threw the pointman into the stone ceiling. Bursts of 9mm fire zipped over Lyons's back, smacked into the chests and faces of the other terrorists. Slugs smashed into the metal of the AK rifles, ricocheted off the stones. As burst after burst twisted the terrorists, Lyons flicked his Colt's fire selector up to single shot and searched for a target.

Dropping his blue flashlight, the last silhouetted terrorist staggered back. Lyons sighted, sent a .45 hollowpoint into the gunman's chest. A burst of 9mm slugs caught the falling man, helped toss out an arm as if he waved goodbye. One slug whined off a wall in the distance.

Groaning came from the walkway. Lyons passed his flashlight back to Gadgets as he whispered, "When you hear me moving, count two, then put some light on them. I'll be up against the side wall."

Slipping an extra magazine from a belt pouch, Lyons held it ready in his left hand. He rose to his feet and groped through the darkness, his shoulder touching the wall as he stepped on corpses and rifles.

A rifle dragged on stone. Gadgets switched on the blue flashlight. It revealed a terrorist reaching for a rifle. Lyons stepped on the clawing hand. He fired a single shot into the dying man's head. He stepped over the others, put single shots into the heads of two others. The pointman did not need such mercy. He had no head.

Checking the corpses, Lyons took the flashlights. Gadgets and Mohammed searched through pockets and found radios. Blancanales reloaded his Beretta, went ahead to the side passage and watched for other terrorists. Mohammed slung his Uzi and took a Kalashnikov. They dumped the bodies into the flowing scum of the sewer.

Blancanales waved them forward. They rushed to the side tunnel. Peering around the corner, they saw a short passage jackhammered through stone and concrete. Light spilled from a rectangle cut above the passageway. A ladder went up the wall to it.

"I heard voices a second ago," Blancanales whispered.

"Think we can chance going in quiet?" Lyons asked.

Boots came down the aluminum rungs. The four Able men pressed themselves flat against the wall. They waited. They heard voices, then another set of boots descending. Blue light swept the walkway.

Two terrorists rounded the corner. The first carried a Kalashnikov and an RPG rocket launcher. The second had a rifle and carried a pack of rockets in fiberboard tubes. Blancanales and Gadgets reached out, put the muzzles of their Berettas against the heads of the terrorists and executed them.

"Shall we take the rockets?" Lyons asked his partners.

"No. There'll be more upstairs." Blancanales took a fragmentation grenade from his battle suit. "We go in loud, yes?"

"Grenades, then the Atchisson." Lyons unslung his full-auto assault shotgun. He checked the safety, tapped the magazine to test the seating, let the weapon hang from his right shoulder. He took out another box mag of 12-gauge shells and jammed it in the back pocket of his slacks.

"Give me a flash bomb," he said. "I've only got one."

"Here you go." Gadgets handed him the grenade. Originally designed for attacking hijackers who held airline passengers hostage, the grenade produced a flash and tremendous concussion that temporarily blinded and stunned but caused no wounds.

Lyons straightened the cotter safety pins. More voices came from the trapdoor. But they heard no feet on the stairs. Lyons glanced around the corner, saw no one.

"On my way." He crept forward, the crunching of his shoes on the walkway's sand the only sound. Motioning Mohammed forward, Gadgets indicated that he and Blancanales would wait at the corner. Mohammed nodded and followed Lyons.

At the foot of the ladder, Lyons jerked the cotter pins from the grenades and held down the levers. A grenade in each hand, he put a foot on the first rung, then shifted his weight slowly. He went up the ladder silently. Below him, Mohammed eased down the safety of his captured AK.

Voices called out. Lyons hurried up the last three rungs, looked up.

Trucks crowded the interior of the cavernous warehouse. Arabs in modern clothes and traditional robes, armed with Soviet AKs and rocket launchers, rushed from truck to truck. They loaded long crates and boxes. Another group of terrorists in dark clothes rushed up a flight of wooden stairs to a second floor. The second floor overlooked the main work and storage area like a mezzanine. A supervisor's windows opened into the warehouse. A corridor went back to other offices. A long flight of stairs led to the roof.

Lyons could not see the American prisoner. He did see a middle-aged Egyptian in elegant evening clothes talking with terrorists. The terrorists bowed as they left the Egyptian.

Letting the levers flip off the grenades, Lyons counted to three, threw the frag toward the elegant Egyptian. The grenade bounced across the concrete. Terrorists turned toward the trapdoor in the floor. Lyons tossed the other grenade, the concussion-flash, then ducked and put his hands over his ears.

An instant after the one-two blast, Lyons went through the trapdoor with his Atchisson in his hands. He scrambled across the floor, crabbed himself under the nearest truck. Jerking the pins from two more grenades—a frag and a flash-blast—Lyons tumbled them under trucks to the other side of the warehouse. He sprayed three shots from his Atchisson at the legs of running terrorists, then cupped his hands over his ears again.

Shock rang in his head. Screaming came from everywhere. Rolling from under the truck, Lyons searched for targets. Lifting an AK, an Arab in a keffiyeh staggered away from a truck. A 12-gauge blast shredded his heart and lungs. On the second floor, the black-clad terrorists fired AK rifles at the trapdoor. Sighting over the Atchisson's fourteen-inch barrel, Lyons snapped single shots into three men. The assault weapon's action locked back.

Dropping the empty magazine, he grabbed the mag in his back pocket. An autorifle fired behind him, slugs roared past his ear. He rolled as three terrorists with AK rifles rushed him, one firing his rifle point-blank into Lyons's chest.

Inside the steel insert and Kevlar of his battle armor the slug's impact felt like a kick. It did not stop his roll. Under the truck again, he jammed the magazine into the Atchisson and slapped the action release with his left hand as he aimed one-handed at the legs of the Arabs.

One terrorist crouched, pointing his AK, as Lyons fired. The fifty high-velocity steel balls tore away the guy's head and the leg of a man behind him. A second blast of steel ripped away the feet of the third man.

Crawling under the driveshaft and springs, Lyons crouched on the far side. He saw Mohammed emerging from the trapdoor, AK in one hand. A terrorist on the second floor rose from cover, pointing his Kalashnikov. The Atchisson ripped him with steel.

Slugs chipped the concrete. Mohammed scurried from the hole, saw Lyons, sprinted a few steps and then dived. An Arab looked from behind a truck, saw Lyons and Mohammed, ducked back. Expecting a rifle barrel or grenade, Lyons sighted on the place where the head had appeared and waited. Beside him, Mohammed snapped two- and three-shot bursts from his Uzi.

The cone point of an RPG appeared in the Atchisson's sights. Lyons fired. The launcher and an arm flew, then the missile streaked straight up.

"Under the truck!" Lyons shouted at Mohammed.

Metal and bits of concrete showered around them,

then whole blocks of concrete and planks fell. Mohammed crawled out and continued to the far side. The sound of boots approached him. He fired his Uzi one-handed, kicked the thrashing terrorist aside. Lyons jerked open a bandolier pouch, found another magazine of seven 12-gauge shells and followed Mohammed out.

The muzzle of an AK appeared in a truck window. Lyons fired through the door's steel, saw blood spray the windshield. He changed mags, looked for more targets.

Autofire hammered the trucks on both sides of them. Glass shattered, a tire blew out. Lyons saw a prone terrorist swing his autorifle toward them. Lyons's snapped shot went low, the double-ought and number two skipping off the concrete, punching into the rifleman's head and torso. The terrorist arced back, flopped down dead.

They heard shouts. The shooting went intermittent then stopped.

Mohammed called over. "The head man's organizing a retreat! That's what he's talking."

Truck engines roared. Lyons crouchwalked to the front of the trucks shielding them. He snapped a glance over the hood, had to duck down as slugs hammered sheet metal and sprayed the plastic and glass of the already shattered windshield.

Chains clanked and pulleys squeaked as a cargo door rose. The street was revealed. Lyons shifted position, tried to sight on whomever operated the pulley and chain to raise the door. Slugs from three autorifles slammed into the truck protecting him.

Searching through his battle armor's pockets, he

found three grenades. As he pulled the cotter pin from the first, he heard gears grind, an engine roar. He threw the grenade blind, wrenched the pin from the next, threw it.

The flat whack of each grenade's hundred sixty grams of explosive sent thousands of steel wires slicing through air and flesh. Lyons chanced another look. No slugs came for an instant. A truck accelerated through the open door. Lyons snapped up his Atchisson and fired a full-auto burst at the driver. Steel balls punched sheet steel.

Slugs from an AK ripped past him and Lyons threw himself flat. Brakes squealed. Another engine roared away as burst after burst of slugs hammered the fenders and tires shielding Lyons. In all, four trucks escaped.

Uzis fired from Lyons's side. He saw Gadgets and Blancanales spraying bursts on the run.

Blancanales crouched beside Mohammed. "Sorry we're late. We had fire coming straight down that hole."

Gadgets jerked the pin from a frag and lobbed it to the second-floor offices. A rifle went silent. A terrorist jumped to his feet with the grenade in his hand and was swinging to throw it back. Blancanales put a burst of 9mm hollowpoints into the terrorist's chest. He fell back into the blast.

Only two Muslim rifles continued firing. Lyons crabbed over to his partners. "I haven't seen the Agency man. And four trucks got out."

Fanning out, firing bursts, Able Team searched through the carnage.

14

THE LINCOLN'S DOOR flew open as the three-ton limousine rocked on its springs. Parks bolted out. Katz and Sadek followed a second later. They ran through the trucks and unmarked Fiats jamming the street in front of the warehouse.

An Agency soldier with overcoat concealing a weapon ran to Parks. "We got some people in there who claim to be highest authority. But they don't have identification or—"

A second CIA soldier rushed forward. "There's one of our men dead. Another missing...."

Parks took the men aside, out of earshot of Sadek and Katz. They spoke quickly, one man pointing to another block, to a car with shattered windows. The second man pointed to a warehouse door. While they spoke, a siren approached. A Cairo police department squad car whipped around a corner, lights flashing. Uniformed officers jumped out, revolvers in their hands.

Parks returned to Sadek. "Something happened here. We don't know what yet. But we need to keep the city police at arm's length until we can sort it out. Can you help us with that?"

"Oh, certainly," sighed Sadek. "But you understand, there will be a full explanation. We operate as allies in this investigation, correct?"

"You have my word. I know nothing about what happened here."

Sadek watched Parks with a calm, knowing expression. "Why do the men inside claim Highest Authority?"

"I have no idea. . . . Please, the police are here."

With a smile, Sadek turned away. Parks watched the Egyptian go to the city officers who stood around, confused. The worried young American turned to Katz. "We got a problem. Come on. . . ."

Motioning Katz to follow, Parks jogged to the guarded street door. The older man, Phoenix Force's scarred and maimed hero, maintained his Foreign Service investigator role as he limped past the Agency men. He gave them a quick salute. They turned their faces away.

Screams echoed in the vast warehouse. Parks started, his head whipping about as he searched the dim interior for the source of the agonized cry. Katz saw a three-story-high area for trucks, then an overhanging second floor of offices. Bodies of Arabs and Africans lay here and there on the oil-blackened concrete. The bitter odors of blood and cordite hung in the air.

Hands stopped Parks. A young Egyptian in a taxi driver's jacket stood in front of them, his outstretched arms pushing them back to the door.

"So sorry, sirs. You not come in. Not allowed."

"Who are you?" Parks demanded.

The taxi driver pressed them back. "So sorry, no speak much English. You not come in."

Again a scream tore the quiet, was suddenly choked off. Then another voice cried out, wailed. Words came. They heard a voice speaking quickly in Arabic, punctuated by shrieks.

Parks stared around the warehouse. His eyes finally registered the corpses strewn around the parked trucks. He shoved past the taxi driver, ran through the trucks.

A knot of men in battle armor clustered around a moaning, thrashing prisoner. Parks attempted to pull two of the armored warriors apart. Lyons jumped to his feet. Grabbing Parks by the shoulders, he threw him against a truck. In a quick sweep of a foot, he hooked Parks's ankles from under him, dropped him to the concrete. He stood over Parks. Blood smeared the black nylon of the hotshot's battle armor and bandoliers.

"You don't interfere in our interrogation. I don't care who you are."

"Highest Authority does not sanction this."

"Those terrorists have an American prisoner. That sanctions everything."

"Craig Parks," Katz told Lyons as he arrived on the scene. "He's temporarily Chief Special Operations Officer."

Parks looked from the oil-smeared face of the blond American to the man he knew as Mr. Steiner. "What's going on here?"

"We're doing your work; now stay out of the way." Lyons went back to the others.

Mohammed translated the Arab's panted, gasped words to Able Team. "...an old agricultural institute three kilometers past el-Minya. Very well defended. Heavy machine guns, mines, wire. Looks like a farm. But it's the fortress of the National Liberation Front."

"Ask him about places in the city here," Blancanales told Mohammed. "Maybe they won't take the American out of the area."

Mohammed questioned the prisoner, listened to the answer. "No, their leader wants the man for bad times. Some of their people went to hideouts in Cairo. But the main force is making it to the desert...."

"You're in with them, aren't you, Steiner?" Parks accused Katz. "What are you really doing? Are you with the Foreign Service?"

"Please be calm," Katz told him.

"Calm! I have a secret team of assassins operating in my area of responsibility. Do you have any idea of what this could do to our relations with this country? When the international news bureaus get this story, the United States will be—"

"Will be nothing!" Lyons interrupted, shouting at the officer. "You're going to tell them? Are you making the call?"

"No! But it's inevitable—"

"Nothing's inevitable," Lyons countered. The warrior slung his Atchisson over his shoulder as the other men left the prisoner.

"We promised to send this guy to a hospital if he helped us. You care so much, Parks, you take care of him."

Tourniquets tied off the Arab terrorist's ankles. Forty-five-caliber slugs had torn ghastly wounds in the man's feet. Behind the moaning prisoner, a dead man lay spread-eagled on the concrete, his feet and hands shot away.

"One talked, the other didn't. Who's he?" Lyons pointed behind Katz.

Sadek watched Able Team straightening their gear. He took a pack of English cigarettes from his coat pocket. He lit a cigarette with a gold lighter.

"Sir, I should ask that of *you*," the Egyptian said.

"Ask him," Lyons pointed to Parks as he moved past Sedak.

The Egyptian watched Able Team and the two taxi drivers jog away. He called after them, "Police and soldiers have surrounded the block. You cannot leave!"

Blancanales called back without breaking pace. "Wanna bet?"

Parks turned to Katz, his face livid. "I'm calling Washington," he said. "You've come here and run your own dirty tricks squad through another country's laws. A country we're attempting to convince of our friendship and respect—"

"Why do you shout at me, Mr. Parks?" Katz asked him.

"Those guys knew you. You were talking with them, they—"

"Talking with whom?" Katz glanced around as if confused by Parks's question.

Parks ran into the open expanse of concrete beyond the parked trucks. His head turned from side to side as he looked for Able Team. He rushed to the nearest trucks, glanced between the vehicles. Katz followed the angry young Agency officer.

"Talking with whom?" Katz repeated.

"They're gone...."

"Who's gone?" Katz asked.

IN THE BACK OF THE PITCHING TRUCK, Jake Newton lay utterly still. Terrorists surrounded him. He felt their boots pressing against his legs, heard the moaning and crying of wounded, the Arabic words of other men.

They ignored him. A minute or so after the terrorists had thrown him into the back of the truck, he had heard the shooting. Slugs and shrapnel had ripped through the canvas. He'd heard the screams and panic, the long firefight. Before he could summon the strength to attempt to escape, hope of rescue had ended as the terrorists crowded into the truck.

Jake faked unconsciousness throughout the long ride from the city. After careering around corners, bumping over the streets of Cairo, every turn and lurch an agony to the battered prisoner, the truck sped through the highway traffic. Which direction had they taken him? It did not matter. He had already cut the rope around his hands. When they stopped, he would try to make his break.

He listened as the truck drove through desert quiet. No traffic passed. The truck neither slowed nor accelerated, simply held a steady speed on a good road. After an eternity, the terrorists around him gathered their weapons and talked again.

Voices called out. He heard the sound of a generator. The truck stopped. He lay still, as if dead, while the terrorists left the truck. A leader shouted instructions in Arabic.

Hands jerked at his feet. As Jake slid from the floorboards of the truck, he pulled his hands from the tangle of ropes on his wrists and opened the one eye that still worked.

Slamming an elbow into a face, feeling teeth break, he grabbed at an AK, felt the stamped metal of the receiver. But he did not have the strength to stand. Blood drained from his head. His legs, still tied at the ankles, buckled beneath him. He fell into darkness before his body hit the ground.

Merciful unconsciousness sheltered the American from the kicks and punches and rifle butts of the Warriors of Allah.

15

BEYOND THE NOISE and streaking headlights of the highway, moonlit fields extended into the distance. Slouched in the back seat of his taxi, Gadgets stared out at the lights of peasant farms and villages. Some lights were the flickering amber of fire, others were electric white. Able Team had left the warehouse as they had entered, through the ancient sewer. Now they raced toward the village of el-Minya.

Would a battle at the old agricultural school end it? All through the night, as they had fought from one terrorist stronghold to another, Gadgets had considered the conflicting and confusing information. He knew the background of the groups, he knew of their involvement in many attacks against moderate Arab leaders and Europeans, he had seen their operations. Able Team had destroyed two separate gangs of Muslim fanatics. Yet he could not think of the night's actions as steps toward victory. The facts simply did not justify optimism.

Keying his hand radio, he buzzed Lyons and Blancanales. "Hey, this is the Wizard. Conference time."

"What do you want to talk about?" Lyons answered.

"All of this trash tonight. It doesn't make sense."

"Tell us," Blancanales told him.

"I want a real conference. We should stop the cabs for a second, all pile into one."

"Why?" Lyons asked. "You think they could monitor our frequency?"

"Not really. I just want to jive face to face. I got a thermos of coffee I'll share."

"Stopping immediately!"

Headlights flashed behind Gadgets and Mohammed. A half-mile back, other high beams blinked. As his taxi eased over to the side of the road, Gadgets saw the other taxis slow and stop. Lyons legged it from his car, Blancanales followed a few seconds later.

Lyons sat in the front seat. He put out a Styrofoam cup. "Where's my coffee? And I didn't come here for any criticism. I think I'm doing great."

"No doubt about it, you're doing fine."

Blancanales swung open the door, caught a Kalashnikov before it fell out. He set the autorifle on the floor and sat next to his partner.

Flooring the accelerator, Mohammed swerved into traffic.

Lyons shouted. "Go easy, you crazy cowboy Arab. The man's pouring my coffee."

Gadgets passed the steaming cup to Lyons, then turned to Blancanales. "You think Mr. Ironman here's doing okay?"

The Puerto Rican ex-Green Beret considered the question, finally answered, "For a leg grunt, yeah."

"What?"

"Yeah," Gadgets agreed. "For a leg soldier, he's got style. Can't complain."

"Hey! I'm not ground bound. I jump. High drop, low drop...."

"With parachute or without," Gadgets added.

"I've jumped. Done it for fun. Don't have jump wings, but.... Talking about tough stuff, where were you when I was rolling around on that killing floor? I got shot waiting for you. Look at this...."

He passed them an AK slug that he had pried out of his battle suit.

Gadgets looked at it. "Did it hurt?"

"Nah, man. Hit me in the—"

"Hit him in the head," Blancanales joked. "Commies should issue armor-piercing rounds when the Ironman comes around."

"Did you want to talk or what?" Lyons demanded, impatient with the kidding.

"Oh, yeah. I don't call a conference to practice my Ironman jokes. About all this stuff with the Raghead International. I been running it through my cranial circuits over and over but it does not make sense. I mean, there's no schematic. It's strictly circle city.

"First, we ran up against that gang who tried to rocket the limousines. We hit them then. Twice. Hard. We went looking for the SAMs, but what do we find? Artillery rockets. Not exactly something you smuggle across the border in a crate marked Farm Tools.

"Then the Agency runs their scam on the jet shooters. They spot one agent in the control tower. But he wasn't the one that alerted the missile crews in the city. They had a radio at the airport communicating with their headquarters in the city. Think about it. They wouldn't have just one man with a buzzer and one man with a voice radio. Ten to one, they got a network of spotters out there at the International.''

Blancanales shook his head slowly. ''That's not certain. Their agent in the tower couldn't radio his information straight, so they had a backup. Makes sense that way, too.''

''Maybe. But look at how they operate in the city. They've got a central command, then satellite units scattered all over the place. The command center got the word, then relayed it to all the other units.''

''Not anymore,'' Lyons told his partner. ''Command Central is deactivated.''

Gadgets gulped his coffee, poured more from the thermos. ''We killed some of them. I checked inside those trucks. Crated SAM-7s and good radios. But you said four trucks got away. And how do we know all of their field units were in the warehouse? Anyway, they hit Air Force planes. Why not American airliners? That's what scares me.''

''We've been chopping arms off the octopus,'' said Blancanales. ''We have to take the head off. But we don't know where the head is.''

''Might have already done it,'' insisted Lyons. ''That one I saw had to be a diplomat. He had the look of an international type. I put an M-67 grenade under him.''

''We didn't find his body,'' Blancanales reminded Lyons.

''I think I got him. Blood all over the place....''

''Blood spots don't make the body count.''

Gadgets cut them off. ''Doesn't matter if that one's alive or dead. I don't think the head was the diplomat the Ironman saw. Dig it, these people have infiltrated *everywhere*. They're in the Egyptian army, in the government, they work at the airport, they're kids on motorbikes. These people are major pros at secrecy. Therefore the head would not have made an appearance at that warehouse. Capture one of his soldiers, you get a description of the leader, you close down the entire operation. My bet is, the head man's some dude no one would suspect. And that's what's kicking me. We have to have a way to close down this operation, not just hack at it."

"What about that Egyptian with the Agency?" Lyons asked.

"I listened in on a conversation between Katz and that Parks guy. They've checked him and checked him. They say he's straight."

"I don't care what they say," Lyons snapped back. "That one saw us. I bet you, and I'll give you even odds, that we get it because of him."

"From Washington?" Blancanales commented. "Don't worry about it."

"I'm not talking about Washington. Now the Egyptians know. I'm saying we could get shat upon out here in the desert."

Gadgets tapped the radio linking Able Team to Katz. "I got a message from the colonel. He's sticking close to that Sadek. He won't let him spill it for a while."

Mohammed shouted out, "El-Minya, two kilometers."

"Time to split up again."

They buzzed their drivers. Gadgets pressed his argument as the taxi slowed. "So we've still got to positively identify the head man. Otherwise we're wasting our time, we're just shooting sand dunes.''

"Tell it to the colonel.'' Lyons gripped the door handle as he waited for the taxi to slow. "We can't do it all.''

Lyons jumped out the door. Dust billowed in the glare of the other taxis' headlights. Blancanales gave Gadgets a salute and stepped out, too. Mohammed waited until the two men got in their cars, then threw the Fiat into gear. "We'll be at the village in about two minutes. Road we want cuts east, into the desert.''

"Go. You're the driver—just go.'' Gadgets flicked on the switch of the high-powered radio unit. Cairo would be at the extreme range of the radio. But he needed to send one last message to Colonel Katz.

BLEARY-EYED ORDERLIES with plastic bags shuffled through the warehouse. Soldiers struggled to descend the stairs with stretchers.

Katz watched Sadek and a technician search through the battle litter. He limped across the warehouse, pausing every few steps. He glanced at weapons the soldiers piled, looked inside trucks, as if evaluating the armament of the terrorists. Edging closer to Sadek, he listened to the Egyptian's comments to the laboratory technician.

"Examine those .45-caliber casings under a microscope,'' Sadek told the technician in Arabic. "Compare the casings to the ones found at the earlier incident. I want it done immediately.''

"The staff will not be there until after nine o'clock in the morning. . . .''

"You will do it. You will do it now—" Sadek turned, saw Katz standing near "—or must I request our American allies to open their facilities? I need a report in an hour."

Dismissing the assistant, Sadek stepped over to Katz. "And what are your conclusions, Mr. Steiner, supposedly of the American Foreign Service?"

"Perhaps it was an industrial accident."

"No. I think not."

"A religious rite? I understand that often what a foreigner mistakes for extremism is actually the expression of a fervent devotion to Allah. Perhaps self-flagellation with whips did not cleanse their souls of guilt, and they used automatic rifles to purge their sins instead . . . with unfortunate consequences."

"Again, I think not."

Katz limped back to Parks. "Assemble your men. We're returning to the embassy."

"What?" Parks asked, feigning surprise. "And leave Sadek here to send coded information to the Communist International?"

Katz smiled at the sarcasm. "Actually, yes."

WIND SWIRLED SAND. In the distance, the lights of the National Liberation Front stronghold blinked in the predawn darkness. Able Team and their "taxi drivers," changed from their street clothes to black night suits, now checked weapons and equipment by the glow of penlights. Lyons loaded Atchisson magazines. Blancanales inspected the rockets and launchers they had taken from dead Muslim terrorists. It would soon be the dawn of another terror-racked day for Mack Bolan's avengers.

They did not prefer their days to be ablaze with terror, any more than Mack Bolan, the rogue supercommander of the U.S. government's leading security enterprise, preferred execution to mercy.

But, like Mack Bolan, his three American freedom fighters known as Able Team knew well enough that somebody had to be true to the way things really were. Somebody had to go beyond mercy and face terror openly, fearlessly, immediately. Somebody had to realize there was no other choice.

Able Team was born of the same fires as Bolan's long-ago Death Squad. The same fires of Mack's own mythical immolation in New York's Central Park that brought The Executioner emerging from ashes as John Phoenix, the greatest counter-terrorist known to man. So Able Team went in blazing. Every time.

They were an extension of Mack's will and yet, out of love and out of duty, they acted entirely independently, unpredictably, for the patriotism of it, for the love known only to the selfless volunteer. It was a high path that shimmered with sacred fires.

They went in blazing, but their enemies cropped up everywhere, unendingly.

Their enemies were the children of the devil, whoever they may be, and there were many. The devil's ilk might be Americans, they might be Chinese, they might be Arab or Jew or Englishman or Congolese, they might be man or woman, very young or very old, but they all identified themselves in one way: their fanatical devotion to destruction for its own sake.

Such destroyers needed a stiff lesson. The lesson

was Able Team. The avenging warriors taught the
ancient law, that for every action—especially
destructive action—there is as powerful a reaction.
For every act—especially the act of taking innocent
life, especially the act of destroying productive
endeavor, especially the act of spilling the blood of
the harmless and wrecking their lives with shock and
horror—there is always an accounting.

Whether you are Jew or Arab or Christian or black
man or preacherman or soldier, your life is in the
care of Mack Bolan and his friends. But if you are of
the devil's party, then the above does not apply. . . .

Mohammed circulated among the others, tucking
frag and flash-blast grenades into empty battle-
armor pockets. Gadgets fitted an earphone to a
captured Muslim walkie-talkie and gave it to
Mohammed.

To protect their throats and lungs against the
blowing sand, Zaki tore a dark shirt into strips and
tied one of the strips over his mouth and nose.
Wordlessly, the others took the makeshift bandan-
nas.

On the crest of a brush-choked sand dune, Abdul
watched the terrorist base through binoculars. His
voice low, he called back to the others, "Sentries.
Searchlights."

Lyons finished with the last box mag of 12-gauge
rounds. He counted the magazines in his bandolier:
fifteen plus one in the weapon—a total of one hundred twelve rounds. He tried walking. With the
weight of the steel-and-Kevlar battle armor, an Armburst rocket, the Atchisson, the modified Colt and
ammunition for both, every step became a conscious

effort. And he had a two-mile march through sand to the base.

Oh, well, could be worse. He could be that American the fanatics had taken prisoner. Was the man still alive? Had the torture started?

Lyons slung the Atchisson and struggled up the dune to Abdul. "What do you see on the perimeter?"

"Look." Abdul passed the binoculars to Lyons.

A searchlight swept the desert, revealing a bulldozed flat ring of sand around barbed-wire fences. Fifty feet of sand separated the fences from the clay walls of the institute.

Lyons slid back down the sandbar and returned to the others.

"What are we up against?" Blancanales asked.

Lyons yawned. "Searchlights, cleared fields of fire, barbed wire, maybe a mine field, ten-foot mud walls, sentries, maybe an army of crazies inside and who knows what else."

"Standard stuff," Gadgets commented. He checked his radio and the radios of the others with a penlight.

In the momentary glows of the light, Zaki and Mohammed looked at the three American commandos, studying their faces for fear or false courage. Despite the odds against them, these Americans appeared at ease.

"But we have the element of surprise," Zaki said as if to bolster his own confidence.

"For now," Gadgets nodded. "But with luck, they'll be expecting us."

"Man, you're kidding!" Mohammed cried out.

"Don't sweat it," laughed Gadgets, "it's part of a plan."

"These dudes are loco," Mohammed muttered to Zaki and Abdul as they followed the hulking shadows of Able Team across the lunarlike desert. "Loco, loco, loco."

16

THEY CROSSED THE OPEN DESERT in a widely spaced skirmish line.

Starlight guided them through the brush dotting the sand. Lyons and Blancanales pressed ahead, scouting for traces of mines or sensors. Gadgets plodded behind with a load of Armburst rockets and a pack of electronics. He stayed close to Mohammed, who monitored the Arabic of the terrorist gang on a captured walkie-talkie.

"Nothing, man," he reported to Gadgets. "Some honcho just checked the guards. Nothing."

Avoiding an area of open sand, Blancanales pushed through weeds, the brittle twigs and dry leaves rasping on his battle armor's nylon. He saw something on the pale sand. He dropped to one knee, swept his eyes across the ground several times, straining to focus in the starlight. He saw several dark objects.

Rocks? No, too small and round. The triggers of some type of ComBloc antipersonnel mines? No, too many. Sensors? Again, too many.

He reached out, touched one, picked it up. A dry goat turd.

Laughing to himself, he continued forward. But the droppings reassured him. Goats wandered in herds. If the fanatics had mined the desert around their fortress, animals would avoid the area. A full half mile of sand and rocks and brush remained ahead of him. He scanned the night for his partners.

A hundred yards to one side, a black form moved through the darkness. In the blowing sand and shifting patterns of gray and black, only the form's relentless pace identified it as Lyons. Blancanales looked back, thought he saw a form against a gray blur of sand, then it dissolved. Forms appeared and disappeared everywhere in his vision.

Very spooky. Which was very good. If the guards had Starlite scopes or infrared viewers, the sandstorm and blowing weeds might make them doubt what they saw. Blancanales checked his watch. Another hour and a half to dawn. Maybe a full hour of night before the sky began to gray.

He squinted at the dust-blurred lights of the fortress. The wind and sand and night would help them get to the fences, but what then?

Lyons wove through the weeds, avoiding open areas that could be mined. His eyes never stopped moving, sweeping from side to side, not focusing, only watching for shapes or movement. He kept his thumb on the safety of his Atchisson, his index finger straight alongside the trigger guard. Cocked and locked. Clenching his fist would send a storm of steel into the night.

The phone plug buzzed in his ear. Gadgets's voice whispered, "Ironman, Politician. Anything interesting?"

"Nah," Blancanales answered.

Touching the transmit key of his radio, Lyons answered without breaking his pace, "Zero."

"Nothing on the party line, either. All quiet ahead."

After three more minutes of steady marching, watching the lights of the fortress become larger, seemingly more brilliant, Lyons dropped to one knee in the brush. He watched the searchlight sweep the fences and the scraped-flat perimeter, its beam blurred with dust. The guard was directing the beam without pattern or rhythm, sometimes bathing the fence in light, sometimes holding it steady on the naked sand, sometimes skimming the beam across the weeds.

Lyons keyed his radio. "I'm about two hundred, two hundred fifty yards away from the wall. We got one very nervous guard up there. He's putting that searchlight everywhere. Time to group and make a plan."

"Guide us to you," Gadgets answered.

One by one, they drifted in from the night and the swirling dust. Crouching shoulder to shoulder, they kept their heads below the weeds. Mohammed continued monitoring the National Liberation Front's frequency.

Blancanales glanced at his watch. "We have less than an hour of night left, depending on how much dust is up in the atmosphere. There's a gully twenty or thirty yards over there. You four will wait there. Ironman and I will dump these rockets and ammo with you, then crawl a circle around the base. Good enough for you?"

Lyons nodded and turned to Gadgets and Mohammed. "Stay on that NLF frequency. We want early warning on any freakout."

"Will do. Let's move."

The men crept the hundred feet to the shallow fold in the desert. Easing over rocks, they sprawled on the sand bottom. Lyons stripped off his bandolier and the Armburst rocket and his battle armor. The wind chilled the sweat-soaked black shirt he wore. With only his radio, silent Colt and a web belt of mag pouches, he crawled toward the lights. Blancanales moved out a minute later, bearing east.

Snaking slowly through the sand, Lyons heard voices on the fortress walls. The searchlight swept the desert, lighting up the gully for an instant. Lyons froze as the light caught him. But it passed. He crabbed to the side, kept one shoulder against the rocks and crumbling sandbank as he continued. The searchlight returned. Lyons froze again, a shadow in the shadows. The beam held on the gully.

The light revealed every rock and ripple of sand, every shatter-pattern of brittle weeds standing black against the glare. Lyons took the opportunity to study the ground in front of him. Only a few yards separated him from the bulldozed-flat zone that surrounded the barbed-wire perimeter fences.

His eyes searched the dirt. A triangle of shallow depressions marked the end of the gully. From one, a curve of rusted iron protruded. A mine. Beyond the gully, Lyons saw depressions in the no-man's-land. Mines. He could not continue forward. Lyons waited as the light swept up and down the gully. Waited for machine-gun fire or darkness.

Darkness came as the beam shifted to the fences.

The light revealed a scrap of plastic sheeting flapping on the wire. Lyons waited for his eyes to readjust, then slithered from the gully. Brush covered him as he continued. He keyed his hand radio. "Pol. They got mines out here."

"I've seen them. Was that light on you?"

"Not really. They're just jerking off up there."

Infinitely slowly, using the light from the fortress walls, Lyons eased through the dry brush. He came to a ridge of rocks and sand and tangled brush plowed aside by the bulldozing of the perimeter clearing. He remembered what Blancanales had taught him. He found a straw-thin twig and swept it ahead of him as he crawled forward. The twig would snag on any trip line without—he hoped—triggering the fuse. Every few feet, he paused to rake his fingers through the sand, searching for the iron of the hubcap-sized mines he had seen. Thorn-sharp dry weeds scratched his hand, rocks cut his knuckles. But scratches did not bother him. Crawling onto a land mine would.

The twig snagged on a line. Studying it in the dim light, Lyons saw a rusted wire. Not monofilament or a strand of almost invisible nylon string, but wire. He followed the wire.

Two Soviet antipersonnel mines stood on the ends of stakes. Rust covered the serrated cast-iron casings. Lyons had followed the wire to the first grenade. Another wire led from the second grenade in the opposite direction. The rust on the cast iron and the green corrosion on the trip-wires indicated months since the placement of the mines.

All this astounded Lyons. A fortress of Muslim

fanatics, the perimeters defended by mines, barbed wire, searchlights and machine guns, less than an hour's drive from downtown Cairo. What did the Egyptian police and military intelligence units do all day? Pose for tourist snapshots?

What if Able Team searched the remote deserts of the country—what would they find? Soviet air bases? The Lost Tribes of Israel? Martian colonies?

A buzz came through his earphones. "Watch for trip lines," Blancanales warned.

"I'm looking at one now. Strictly junk...."

"Which could blow you away."

"I'm not going to deactivate them. We don't have the time."

Blancanales bellied past a pair of Soviet bombs. Every few yards, he stopped to watch the sentries on the walls. Silhouetted against the night sky or lighted by the reflected glare of the searchlight, they paced aimlessly. Some stood in one place for minutes, smoking cigarettes or talking.

Examining the bare expanse of the minefield, Lyons saw no path to the fence. The small depressions where the sand had settled marked most of the mines. But crossing the no-man's-land would require slow, meticulous probing of every square foot of sand while the searchlight sought out intruders. After that, they faced the eight-foot-high tangle of barbed wire, then a second minefield before they reached the ten-foot-high clay walls.

Wind brought snatches of Arabic from the wall. Blancanales crept through the brush, blown dust and dry weeds masking his small sounds and movement. The searchlight swept erratically over the sand and brush. Blancanales sometimes went flat, motionless as the light passed over him, sometimes used the light to scan the sand for mines or trip lines.

He rounded the corner of the fortress. Now his eyes searched the south wall. Sentries paced the top of the wall. An unused searchlight stood on a pedestal. Floodlights illuminated gates of riveted sheet steel. On each side of the gates, walled sentry positions guarded the approach to the fortress. The muzzles of heavy machine guns protruded from the positions.

Finally, he came to asphalt. Tangles of barbed wire fenced both sides of the entry road, two lanes wide. Floodlights lighted the approach.

No good. No way in but the road. Blancanales thought of the assault on the fortress of Wei Ho. Only surprise and luck gave Able Team that victory. He remembered the image of Lyons, smeared with genipap body-blacking, his Atchisson bouncing on his back, sprinting into a cross fire, vaulting the gate as AK slugs whined past him. Lyons had made it because no sane man would have risked the gate. The next man over, a Xavante warrior brave beyond understanding, had taken AK hits in the chest and leg. But that was another action, another time....

No frontal attack this time. Blancanales believed God gave men only a certain amount of luck. Lucky once, twice, three times, great. Don't depend on it. He'd seen a lot of young men die who had thought they had good luck. Rushing the gate of the Muslim fortress with six men—even with rockets and grenades—would be to hope for infinite luck.

Keying his hand radio, he buzzed his partners.

"I'm at the gate. South wall. We got to rethink this. There's no way in."

"I'm all the way to the east wall," Lyons added. "Don't see any way over the wall. Guess we have to go straight in...."

"Hey, Carl. No way. Maybe tomorrow night. Maybe we can borrow a helicopter from the air force."

"That's too late. There's an American in there! He won't be alive tomorrow. The terrorists will cut him to pieces tonight. We go in...."

"Don't even think it!" Blancanales snapped back. "It would be suicide. You think you're immortal? I'm looking at a steel gate. Two heavy-caliber machine guns. Sentries with rifles looking down on a road as naked as a baby's ass."

"Relax, Pol," Gadgets whispered, trying to calm him. "We'll just have to sedate the wild man if he tries it."

Lyons came on again. "How about driving one of the taxis up to the gate? We could blast it open with rockets...."

"We don't know that the man's still alive. If he's already dead, we'd all die for nothing. The mission first. Even that poor son of a bitch in there would tell you that."

After a long pause, Lyons agreed. "All right. We're pulling back."

Sprawled flat in the gully, Gadgets heard the microrecorder in his backpack click on. He felt the vibration of the tiny motors reeling the miniature cassette. Whispering into his hand radio, he told the others, "Lay cool for a minute. Wizard's got a plan in gear...."

Reaching across the gully to Mohammed, Gadgets hissed, "You listening to that Arabic station?"

"Oh, yeah, man. Listening to the Raghead Rock.... Hey! It's a Red Alert! They know we're out here! They're scrambling trucks!"

Gadgets laughed quietly.

Several hundred yards away, Lyons heard shouting in the fortress. He saw sentries running along the walls.

Reaching to key his hand radio, Blancanales whispered from his earphone, "There's a truck coming out the gate. And a searchlight just came on! What do you have on that captured radio? What's going on?"

Mohammed whispered a translation to Gadgets. "The man's sending a squad out to search the desert. Another squad's setting an ambush on the road. They just got word that we're on our way. Dig it! Someone's told them we're coming!"

"But we're already here..." Gadgets laughed quietly, keying his radio. "Things are changing. I think we'll get our chance."

The truck roared past a prone Blancanales. He saw the gates close. Raising himself to a crouch, he observed the truck stop a quarter-mile away. In the red glow of brake lights, he noted soldiers in black uniforms leave the truck. He counted ten flashlights. The flashlights were extinguished as the soldiers left the road and fanned out into the desert. The truck pulled away and continued toward the village.

"Hey, Wizard," Blancanales whispered into his radio, "I don't know what your plan is, but the gate's closed, and they just cut off our retreat. If they find the taxis, they'll know—"

"Hold on! Something else is going on. . .just a second. . .we're listening in.... Just wait...."

The gates swung open again. More headlights appeared. Two trucks left the fortress in low gear, heading toward Blancanales. The first truck slowed, the second truck stopped only twenty feet away. Blancanales crabbed backward, putting more distance and brush between himself and the soldiers who would be coming out of the truck. He paused to send out a warning on his radio. "Pull out! They sent out two more truckloads of crazies. They'll be combing the perimeter—"

Lyons broke in on the frequency. "There are lights all over the place! It looks like...."

To the east, parallel lines of white lights lighted the desert.

17

SURVEYING THE FORTRESS from the door of his office, Omar watched his soldiers rush to their posts. His faithful manned the Soviet 12.7mm machine guns guarding the approach to the gate. Other soldiers with rifles and rocket launchers crouched at the wall, looking down at the desert. Any American agents who dared attack his headquarters would meet death below the walls.

"Commander!"

Omar turned to his assistant. To insure instantaneous and accurate communications, Omar had stationed his communications technicians and their equipment in an outer room of his offices. Only a door separated him from the electronics linking him to Cairo, Tripoli, Damascus, Moscow. And Allah had rewarded his foresight tonight. Seconds after receiving warning of the gang of American assassins, he had alerted his officers and soldiers.

The young Libyan who manned the radios slipped off his headphones, called out, "The squads are in position."

"Good."

A soldier ran into the offices. "Commander. The prisoner is conscious."

"Oh?" Omar smiled at the thought. Now he

JOIN FORCES WITH THE EXECUTIONER AND HIS NEW AVENGERS!

THE EXECUTIONER

MACK BOLAN LIVES IN EXPLOSIVE ALL-

He learned his deadly skills in Vietnam…then put them to good use by destroying the Mafia in a blazing one-man war. Now **Mack Bolan** is back to batt new threats to freedom—and he's recruited some high-powered avengers to help…**Able Team**—Bolan's famous Death Squad from Vietnam—now reborn to tackle urban savagery too vicious for regular law enforcement. And **Phoenix Force**—five extraordinary warriors handpicked by Bolan to fight the dirtiest of anti-terrorist wars around the world.

In the forefront is Mack Bolan himself, the Executioner, waging his single-handed war on the enemies of justice and democracy wherever they hide.

Fight alongside these three courageous forces for freedom in all-new, pulse-pounding action-adventure novels! Travel to the jungles of South America, the scorching sands of the Sahara desert, and the desolate mountains of Turkey. And feel the pressure and excitement building page after page, with non-stop action that keeps you enthralled until the explosive conclusion! Yes, Mack Bolan and his avengers are living large…and they'll fight against all odds to protect our way of life!

Now you can have all the new Executioner novels delivered right to your home!

You won't want to miss a single one of these exciting new action-adventures. And you don't have to! Just fill out and mail the card at right, and we'll enter your name in the Executioner home subscription plan. You'll then receive four brand-new action-packed books in the Executioner series every other month, delivered right to your home! You'll get two **Mack Bolan** novels, one **Able Team** book and one **Phoenix Force.** No need to worry about sellouts at the bookstore…you'll receive the latest books by mail as soon as they come off the presses. That's four enthralling action novels every other month, featuring all three of the exciting series included in the Executioner library. Mail the card today to start your adventure.

FREE! Mack Bolan bumper sticker.

When we receive your card we'll send your four explosive Executioner novels and, absolutely FREE, a Mack Bolan "Live Large" bumper sticker! This large, colorful bumper sticker will look great on your car, your bulletin board, or anywhere else you want people to know that you like to "live large." And you are under no obligation to buy anything—because your first four books come on a 10-day free trial! If you're not thrilled with these four exciting books, just return them to us and you'll owe nothing. The bumper sticker is yours to keep, FREE!

Don't miss a single one of these thrilling novels…mail the card now, while you're thinking about it. And get the Mack Bolan bumper sticker FREE as our gift!

hoped the assassins came. The screams of their compatriot would greet them.

Following the soldier into the night and the blowing dust, Omar hurried along the wide balcony in front of the offices. Once students and professors crowded the rooms and hallways of this fortress, studying modern irrigation and biotechnical crop engineering. Grants from the United Nations had helped build the institute, helped pay the professors, helped provide scholarships to the students. With the rise of Omar's power, his movement had taken the classrooms for barracks, the offices for their commanders. The United Nations still funded the institute.

Rushing down the stone steps, Omar and a soldier went to the tiny room where they had thrown the American. He lay on the floor, his hands tied behind him, a loop of rope pulling his hands and feet together. Blood pooled on the tiles, bubbled around the man's ruined mouth. Omar stood over the prisoner for a moment and listened to the man's ragged breathing.

He kicked the American in the stomach. The breathing caught, blood sprayed from the man's mouth. But he did not move or groan. Omar kicked him in the face again and again. No movement.

"The dog! He'll die before we can take our amusement."

Omar kicked him a last time and started back to his office. He glanced at the number glowing on his digital watch. Any moment now, he would receive the coded message announcing the latest delivery of gifts from the Soviets.

The Libyan radioman looked up from his electronics. "The shipment arrives in two minutes."

The missiles! More weapons for the Jihad. Weapons, if need be, to start World War III.

SPRAWLED FLAT IN THE SAND, trapped between the lights of the fortress and the lines of lights in the desert, Lyons heard aircraft engines coming from the east. *That explains it,* he thought. *There's an airstrip out there.*

Gadgets's voice came through his earphones. "Be cool, Ironman. Those lights aren't for you. There's a flight coming in."

"You hear the engines?" Lyons whispered into his radio.

"Oh, man, we're hearing everything. We got those crazies wired—"

Blancanales interrupted. "The trucks are moving out, cutting to the east."

"That's a squad to unload the plane," Gadgets added.

"This is it," Lyons told them. "Those trucks are the ticket. Wizard, Pol, all you other guys circle around. We'll ride right through those gates. Bring my gear. I'm on my way to wherever those trucks park."

"Moving!"

Keeping his belly to the sand, Lyons slithered east. After a hundred feet, he crawled, keeping his back below the swaying brush. Stones tore his knees and hands. Only when the windstorm's dust screened him from the sentries did he rise to a crouch. Behind him, the searchlights swept the perimeter, their beams brown smears against the night. Ahead, he saw the high beams of the trucks nearing the desert airstrip.

Wing lights came from the sky. Prop noise roared. A black-painted cargo plane of a type Lyons did not recognize bounced over the sand. When the plane slowed to taxi speed, the airstrip's lights went dark.

Lyons jogged through the blackness. The wind whipped grit into his eyes. Blinking it away, wiping his eyes with his hands, he did not break pace. In front of him, working by the plane's lights, the crew and the terrorist squad secured a ramp from a side door. The plane's props turned at minimum rpm.

Machine-gun fire! Lyons dropped flat, keyed his hand radio. "Wizard! Pol! What goes?"

Heavy slugs tore the night. Muzzle-flashes sparked from the walls of the fortress. Gadgets and Blancanales and their three taxi drivers watched the terrorists spray fire into the desert hundreds of yards away from them. Mohammed listened to the captured walkie-talkie. "They think they see Americans, but—"

An RPG shrieked, exploded. The autofire from the machine guns and Kalashnikovs died away.

"Their man's telling them to hold their fire. He's trying to find out who saw what."

Blancanales laughed, answered Lyons, "They're shooting at shadows."

"Get over here," Lyons answered. "They're unloading the plane. Move it!"

They ran in a wide circle around the perimeter, the weight of their weapons slowing them. Again, machine-gun fire hammered at the desert, this time on the far side of the fortress. The autofire continued, then died away as officers brought their soldiers under control.

Approaching the parked plane and trucks, Blancanales signaled the group to halt. He keyed his radio. "Ironman, where...."

A shadow crouched beside them. "Good thing they don't put sentries out here," Lyons told them. "Would've got you...."

"Here is your equipment," Zaki told him, passing Lyons his battle armor and bandolier. Abdul unslung the heavy Atchisson.

Lyons slipped into his gear. He pressed closed the Velcro strips, belted the bandolier tight across his body. He slung the Atchisson over his back and pulled the sling tight. He gave the Armburst rocket to Abdul to carry.

"Pol, Wizard, lighten up. We go in first with the pistols." Lyons sketched out a plan in whispers. "The plane's still got its engines going. I figure they'll take off the second they get it unloaded. I say we get close, wait for the first chance, rush the ragheads in the back of the second truck. If we can do it without the driver of the first truck knowing, that's the way through the gate. What do you say?"

"And the taxi boys?" Blancanales asked.

"Use them for backup. If things come apart, they put down the soldiers in the first truck. If absolutely necessary. That would totally blow it. Then it'd be down to crashing the gate."

"What about that plane?" Gadgets asked. "Shame to let it go."

"Can't do it all," Lyons answered. "Number one priority is to get through that gate."

"You're still talking like a kamikaze," Blancanales muttered.

Gadgets laughed quietly. "Hey, Pol, pray for luck."

"Let's go," Lyons said as he crouchwalked toward the trucks.

It took a moment to shift loads. Gadgets's radios and electronics, the rockets, the Kalashnikovs and ammunition went to Abdul, Mohammed and Zaki. Then they trotted after Lyons.

A hundred yards from the trucks and plane, Lyons went to his hands and knees. With the scrub brush concealing him, he scrambled forward until he heard the voices of the soldiers loading the trucks. He went even flatter to snake through the blowing sand and weeds.

Raising his head, he saw soldiers passing long crates from man to man down the ramp to the trucks. A soldier paced the airstrip, staring out at the desert. Lyons waited for Gadgets and Blancanales to catch up with him. They continued forward.

Now they moved even more slowly, carefully, pushing brush and windblown weeds aside with a care previously devoted to trip lines. They came to a ridge of sand and rocks scraped off the desert when the airstrip had been created. Lyons eased his head up.

Only twenty feet away, the sentry paced. His eyes swept the desert to the south. The distant popping of autofire came from the fortress. The sentry glanced to the west, then called out to the truck. A soldier with a radio shouted an answer. The sentry resumed his pacing.

At the plane, the soldiers jumped off the cargo ramp. The flight crew pulled the ramp inside the plane. Two soldiers slid the last crate into the back of the second truck. The other soldiers crowded into the first truck. The sentry ran to join the others.

A hundred feet of open ground separated Able Team from the second truck.

"We got to chance it," Lyons hissed. He slipped out his silenced Colt.

Blancanales's hand caught his arm. "Wait a second."

The plane's engines roared, the props fanning a vast cloud of dust as the plane taxied away from the trucks. A swirling wall of impenetrable darkness swept over Able Team.

Breaking from cover, they sprinted for the truck, the dust concealing them, the engine noise covering the sound of their boots.

Squinting through the prop-storm, Lyons saw the taillights of the truck. He saw the form of the sentry, his Kalashnikov slung over his shoulder, climbing into the truck. Lyons stepped up behind him, waited until the man got up. Lyons raised his left hand for help.

Gripping Lyons's hand, the terrorist pulled him up. A .45 slug smashed through his face, sprayed his brains over the soldiers sitting on the crates. Lyons leveled the Colt, fired a hollowpoint slug into the chest of each astounded terrorist, one-two-three, shock slamming their bodies back. They fell to the floor, two still moving, blood-choked noises coming from their throats. One struggled to pull a pistol from a belt holster. Lyons shot all three in the head, jammed another magazine into his pistol. Only ten seconds had passed.

The truck's diesel engine revved. Lyons turned as a breathless Blancanales and Gadgets climbed in. They reached back, pulled up the three panting taxi drivers and their heavy loads of weapons. Crowding the back of the truck, the men unslung their weapons and checked loads.

The truck accelerated away.

"Did it, man!" Gadgets grinned. "You did it!"

Another form rushed from the swirling dust. The AK-47 in one hand, he grabbed the side of the truck and jumped up to the bed. Blancanales and Lyons shot him simultaneously. He flopped back, dead before he disappeared into the dust that clouded behind the truck.

"Don't celebrate yet," Lyons hissed. "The trip's just starting."

"Don't I know it," Gadgets replied. He hinged down the grips of an Armburst missile to arm the weapon. He held it ready.

Bouncing and swaying as the truck turned onto the desert road and back to the fortress, the six men readied their weapons. Lyons pulled the magazine out of his Atchisson, ejected the round from the chamber, then checked the action for sand. He blew out the receiver, snapped back the actuator several times, finally reloaded the full-auto assault shotgun. He slapped the pockets of his battle armor to count grenades. He slipped box mags of 12-gauge rounds into each thigh pocket of his blacksuit.

Blancanales, Gadgets and the taxi men all had Uzis. Looping the Uzis' slings over their backs, they strapped the cocked and locked 9mm submachine guns against their chests. They checked captured AKs, stripped more ammunition from the dead men on the floor of the truck. Mohammed took a roll of heavy tape from one of his pockets and taped banana magazines of 7.62mmx39 ComBloc ammo end to end. Quickly, all of the AKs had sixty-round loads.

Squatting, Lyons searched through the pockets of the dead men. He found Soviet frag grenades. Shaped like stubby beer cans, the grenades had fuse assemblies protruding from the top. Lyons straightened all the cotter pins, passed some to Blancanales and Gadgets. "When we're inside, all at once."

Brakes squealed as the trucks stopped at the gate. In the back of the second truck, sitting on crates of highly explosive SAM-7 missiles, they waited. Weapons hung by slings from every man—rockets, AK autorifles, Uzis.

Voices shouted in Arabic. The gates clanked open. As the seconds slipped away, Able Team and their three colleagues waited—silent, alone with their thoughts.

Blancanales looked to the east and saw a gray smear through the blowing sand. He crossed himself.

Lurching into motion again, the truck entered the fortress.

18

As the steel gates creaked closed, autofire shattered the quiet. Voices shouted in Arabic. The reflexes of the six men in the back of the truck threw them into action. The taxi drivers hit the floor, Gadgets and Blancanales jolted for the tailgate. Lyons waved them back. They realized no slugs had hit the truck. The gunners on the walls were not directing the fire at the commandos inside the fortress. Lyons looked up and saw terrorists on the walls firing out at the desert's night shadows and wisps of blowing sand. An officer scanned the perimeter with an infrared viewer.

"This is *it*," Lyons told the others. He pointed to the 12.7mm heavy machine guns. "Wizard, Moman. Rockets."

Lyons jerked the safety pin from the first Soviet fragmentation grenade. He bounced it off the east wall, pulled another pin, threw that grenade to the west as Blancanales and Zaki did the same.

Then the Armburst rockets shriekroared, their counter-mass blowing free in a flurry of plastic chips. The machine-gun positions with their stacks of cartridge boxes and three-man crews disappeared in sprays of flame before the direction of the rockets was apparent. Grenade explosions swept the wall top, left only blood and broken stone. Lyons leaped from the tailgate. Throwing down the spent rocket tubes, Gadgets and Mohammed followed him. Blancanales, Zaki and Abdul shouldered launchers, fired rockets from the truck at the terrorist soldiers crowding the south wall of the fortress. Frenzied autofire swept the desert in search of the attackers.

Fanning out from the truck, Lyons, Gadgets and Mohammed saw a central courtyard jammed with vehicles. Headlights and strings of electric bulbs lighted the courtyard.

Clouds of dust and smoke descended from the blasted walls and enveloped the intruders, concealing them as the source of an attack that could only be coming from where it was predicted to come from— out in the desert. Soldiers ran everywhere—between the trucks, along the walls, from the doorways of the rooms lining the courtyard. None fired at the intruders in their midst. Some ran right past Lyons and Gadgets.

Mohammed raised his AK. Lyons motioned him to hold his fire. Lyons let his Atchisson hang on its sling and slipped out his silenced Colt. The others jumped from the truck. Blancanales held the last Armburst, Abdul a loaded RPG-7 launcher and a bandolier of rockets.

Lyons called out to them, "Up the stairs! To the wall!"

Gunmen directed continuous autofire at imaginary Americans attacking from the desert. Terrorists ran to the south wall, searched through the smoking debris. Running up the stone steps, Lyons saw a young African stare at his face.

Recruited in a village in Angola by Cuban cadres, Soyo Neta had marched in the guerrilla bands raiding Namibian farms, slaughtered villagers while serving in the Expeditionary Forces of Libya, then worked as a sniper in Beirut, earning seventy-five American dollars a day murdering Christians who strayed into his field of fire. For years, Cubans, Libyans, Palestinians, East German instructors and officers had preached the destruction of the United States. Now he faced an American. Fear twisting his gut, bile rising in his throat, the African mercenary lifted his AK.

A .45 slug slammed through his chest, destroying his heart and left lung. He staggered back, his vision going dark, all the slogans and chants and prayers of his Soviet/Muslim indoctrination in terror spinning through his panicked mind. His lips formed a last word, but his dead lungs had no breath as he fell into the void.

Another terrorist struggled to lift a legless comrade from the wall's wide walkway. Gadgets snapped 9mm slugs into the heads of the Arabs.

Lyons turned to Blancanales and Abdul. "Hit the truck with the rockets!"

"Take cover!" Blancanales shouted. He sprawled on his belly to sight on the truck below them. The others went flat against the outer wall as the rocket slammed into the cargo of SAM-7 antiaircraft missiles.

The blast shattered the truck, sent a churning ball of flaming diesel fuel upward. Missiles flew wild, ripped into trucks, exploded against walls, pinwheeled high into the sky. Flames rose from burning trucks. A car exploded, the gasoline spraying liquid flame over other vehicles. A burning terrorist ran screaming from the inferno.

Flame and gutted hulks blocked the fortress gates.

Lyons called out to Blancanales and Gadgets, "Pistols first! Until they catch on...."

Two Arabs in the patterned keffiyehs of the Palestine Liberation Organization ran up the stairs. Nine-millimeter slugs from Blancanales's silenced Beretta 93-R punched through their hearts.

Able Team and its allies crept to the east wall. They stayed close against the wall where the choking black smoke hid them from the gunmen on the opposite walls.

An officer ran through the smoke and flames, pushing the weapons of his soldiers, attempting to bring the wild autofire under control. He spoke into his walkie-talkie, listened for a moment. He directed three soldiers to the south wall. The AK-armed terrorists ran directly into Blancanales's Beretta. He put steel-cored 9mm subsonic slugs into their chests.

Lyons motioned Abdul forward. "Have a rocket ready. Sweep the wall when I signal...."

Abdul went to one knee and sighted his RPG-7 on the line of terrorist riflemen firing into the shadows and darkness of the windstorm. Mohammed, Zaki and Gadgets cleared away from the back of the launcher.

Lyons sighted between the shoulder blades of the shouting officer, snapped his spine with a hollowpoint. The officer flopped to the stone, flailing his arms for a moment before his last breath sprayed blood from his throat. Terrorists rushed to the dead man. Forty-five-caliber and 9mm slugs from the silenced autopistols dropped them. The screams pierced even the cacophony of the autofire and exploding fuel in the courtyard.

The line of terrorists manning the wall turned. Some saw a wounded man staggering drunkenly with his hands to his shattered face. Others saw the group of black-clad soldiers crouching at the corner of the walls. Kalashnikovs pointed at Lyons.

"Hit them with the rocket!" he roared.

Slugs tore past Abdul as he pulled the RPG's trigger. A brilliant flash ripped the east wall. Abdul reloaded the launcher and looked to Lyons for a command.

Gripping his Colt with both hands, Lyons searched for living terrorists. Screams and moans came from the twisted debris. A terrorist clawed at the wall tiles, tried to crawl away from the horror of what had been his lower body. Lyons snapped a silent hollowpoint slug into his head and ran forward.

A dying Palestinian clutched a Kalashnikov. A .45 slug ended his suffering. The Colt's action locked back, and Lyons paused to drop the empty mag and slap in another. Blancanales charged past him after two terrorists running up a flight of stone steps. Two bursts of 9mm slugs spun them and sent them rolling down the steps.

A central building met the east wall, doors and windows opening to a roofed walkway. Other windows opened to the wall's walkway. The roof walkway continued around the building to the north wall. An autorifle fired from the corner, slugs gouging the wall near Abdul.

Mohammed, who still monitored the terrorists on the captured walkie-talkie, shouted to his compatriots, "They know! They're getting it together to waste us!"

Unaimed AK slugs tore through the smoke, punched the walls as gunmen on the west wall fired blind. Holstering his Colt, Lyons sprinted to the windows. He pulled a grenade from one of his battle armor's pouches and tossed it through the window. The blast sprayed glass. He looked up to the roof to see the form of a sentry silhouetted against the graying sky. A second grenade went up to the roof. An instant after the blast, a body fell to the walkway. Lyons finished the wounded man with a stomp on the throat. Then he signaled the others to join him.

"Abdul! The corner. Sweep that north wall!"

An Arab keffiyeh bobbed at the corner. Blancanales brought up his Beretta, waited an instant. When the headdress and a Kalashnikov appeared, he sprayed a three-shot burst into the Palestinian's face. Blancanales tore the pin from a grenade, let the lever flip away as he ran to the corner. He pitched it, then motioned Abdul forward.

The grenade sent steel wire zipping through the air. Abdul did not risk exposing himself to sight the missile. Extending the launcher at arm's length, he pointed the rocket around the corner and fired. A roar-flash shook the building. He reloaded the launcher even as bits of stone and metal rained down.

Autofire from the opposite wall raked the deserted walkway of the east wall. The smoke and swirling soot concealing Able Team also hid the gunmen.

Lyons grabbed Gadgets and Mohammed. "The roof! Boost me up."

Lyons stood on his partners' shoulders to grab the edge of the wall. He scanned the rooftop for a moment, then swung his legs over. An AK flashed.

Shock slammed Lyons against the wall. Slugs searched for him, bits of clay and whitewash falling on him as he scrambled away. He tore his Colt from its holster to trigger a three-shot burst at the muzzle-flashes. He saw a rifle fall to one side. Sighting at a form sprawled on the rooftop, he fired again and saw a piece of a gunman's skull fly away.

Lyons unslung his Atchisson before searching for his wound.

He felt no pain. Feeling his shoulders and back, he thought perhaps his battle armor had stopped the slug. Then his hand touched a gouge in the plastic foregrip of the Atchisson. The slug had only scored the plastic.

Leveling the Atchisson, Lyons flicked off the safety and rose to a crouch. He checked a body, found it was a Palestinian girl. Her back was spotted with tiny wounds from his grenade's steel wire fragments. Lyons searched her bloodsoaked uniform and came up with Soviet grenades. Going to the edge, he helped pull Blancanales to the roof.

"Thought you were gone," Blancanales told him.

"Me, too." Lyons leaned over the edge and shouted to the others, "Watch that patio. Watch the north wall. Pol and I will put some fire down their throats."

Gadgets put a burst of Uzi fire into a terrorist rushing up the stairs. A grenade bounced across the ground. Mohammed kicked it as the others dropped flat. The Soviet frag tumbled down the stone steps and exploded in the courtyard.

Lyons sighted his Atchisson on yet another form silhouetted by flames. He killed the terrorist, then followed Blancanales to the north. Below them, autofire hammered.

Chancing a glance over the edge, Blancanales saw two soldiers behind a sandbagged searchlight position who were firing at Abdul. In front of the gunmen, only torn bodies and blood pools remained of the terrorists hit by the rocket. Taking a grenade from his thigh pocket, Blancanales jerked out the cotter pin and let the lever sail free. He counted to three, dropped the frag and pulled his head back to safety. The grenade exploded in the air three feet above the terrorists. High-velocity steel shards reduced their heads to pulp.

Another terrorist broke from cover, screaming, an arm hanging limp. He ran for the west wall. A terrorist stuck an RPG around the corner and fired. The rocket hit the wounded man in the chest. It vaporized his upper body.

Pulling out more grenades, Lyons and Blancanales ran to the west. They pulled the pins. Blancanales said, ''Now....'' The levers flipped away. ''One, two, three—over they go!''

Simultaneous blasts cleared the corner. Lyons leaned over the roof's low wall and snapped semiauto 12-gauge shots into every terrorist he saw, emptying his magazine in less than two seconds. He ducked back as AKs popped. Slugs chipped the wall and whined into the sky.

Keying his hand radio, he shouted, "North wall's clear...."

An explosion knocked the two of them flat. Stone showered them. A section of the wall edging the roof had disappeared.

Lyons found the radio and shouted, "Hit the west wall! They're hitting us!" He jammed the radio back in a pocket and helped Blancanales to his feet. "How many grenades you got left?"

"Haven't been counting...."

A round grenade arced toward them. Lyons lunged forward and whacked the grenade with the plastic stock of his Atchisson, sending it down into the courtyard's inferno. A rocket shrieked over them and continued high into the sky, where it exploded. Lyons dropped the empty box mag out of his Atchisson and jammed in another. "This is getting serious."

Blancanales jerked the pin from a grenade and looked for a target. Kalashnikovs flashed. He dodged back, blindly tossing the grenade. Lyons counted to three and crouchwalked forward. When he heard the bang of the grenade, he stood up and sprayed three riflemen with high-velocity steel shot.

A terrorist with an RPG had leaned from cover and was sighting on Lyons. Lyons sighted on the terrorist's face. The Able Team hotshot squeezed off a burst. One hundred sixty double-ought and number two steel balls riddled the terrorist and his launcher. One of the steel pellets crushed the rocket's electronic fuse cap. The explosion left twenty feet of the walkway a smoking ruin.

Terrorists scrambled from cover. Blancanales

sighted on a form, saw the rifleman disappear off the wall. Another terrorist jumped off the wall to the sand outside the fortress. A second later, a mine exploded, throwing a leg into the air.

Rifle fire came in bursts from isolated positions. A rocket flash swept the west wall. Lyons ran to the northwest corner and looked down at Abdul reloading his launcher. "The south wall! Clear it!"

"You got it, Yank! Cover me."

Dashing around the corner, Abdul sighted on the muzzle-flashes. The flash destroyed a sandbagged searchlight and silenced an AK.

The building heaved beneath Lyons's feet as a rocket came from a concealed terrorist. The charge blasted through the exterior wall. Abdul sighted on the rocket man's hiding place and hit it.

Lyons keyed his radio again. "Wizard. The enemy is retreating, holing up. We got to find that Agency man."

"There are still the squads outside. They'll come back."

"I doubt it. If they do, let them try the minefield."

Blancanales aimed single shots down at forms in the graying predawn. Slugs killed wounded, punched more wounds in the dead. No shots answered Blancanales's methodical fire. Finally, nothing moved on the walls.

"Now search the place," Lyons told his partner.

"After we find our man, we pull out," Blancanales said. "We're pushing our luck way too far."

"No argument from me...."

Going to the roof's edge, they signaled to Abdul below. Lyons lowered Blancanales to Abdul's shoulder, then Abdul and Blancanales helped Lyons down.

In the courtyard, fires still burned in the gutted hulks of the trucks and cars. Dead and dying terrorists were sprawled everywhere. Human debris littered the walkways, the tiles slick with blood. Above the desert, the first pink light of day streaked the sky.

Able Team moved through the wreckage and death, searching for the American prisoner of the National Liberation Front.

19

HIDING IN A CLOSET, Omar shook with fear. The darkness of the tiny space stank of the urine fouling his fatigues. Ashamed of his fear of martyrdom, yet fearing capture more than death, the commander thought of suicide, to die with his men rather than accept the shame of trial.

Or interrogation. Were the attackers Egyptian commandos? If his countrymen took him, there was no hope. He would be dismembered as a matter of course. Unless he had enough gold to buy his freedom.

Or were they American? By radio from Cairo, his leader had warned him. It had been the Americans who had attacked his command center in the city. Did they now search for the American he had captured? What treatment could he expect? He thought of suicide, his body shaking at the thought.

Should he rush from hiding? Throw himself at the attackers? Offer his life to Allah?

Despite his terror, he laughed at these possibilities. He talked like that to his soldiers. He talked of Allah and martyrdom and Paradise, but he knew only graves awaited dead soldiers—sometimes not only graves, only places by the side of the road, a feast for green-backed flies.

But what if Americans found him?

Forcing himself to face the chance of death, he realized he feared death less than capture by the Americans. And even if he fought, death might not come quickly. Fumbling in the thigh pocket of his tailored fatigues, he found a grenade. He looped a finger through the safety pin.

If Egyptians found him, he would surrender and trust his luck to his compatriots' fickleness.

If Americans found him—the determined Americans—he would give himself a quick death and take the Americans with him.

IN THE FIRST GRAY LIGHT OF DAY, nothing moved. Flames flickered in the courtyard. Soot-heavy smoke rose in swirls as the dying wind whipped the flames. Somewhere a wounded man screamed and whimpered.

"We can't go room to room," Blancanales told Lyons. "We'd run into every one of those losers who are still alive."

"I know all about it. Number one cop fear: searching rooms with lowlifes waiting to kill you."

"If we can find one alive, one who'll tell us where our man is. . . ."

Lyons laughed. "Then we got to search these rooms. Let's go." He keyed his hand radio. "Wizard!"

Gadgets jogged around the corner. "What you want?"

"See any of these losers alive?"

"I hear one." He pointed toward the sound of the screaming man.

"Get the others organized. We got to find that Agency man. If we can find a raghead who knows where, that'll get us out of here quick."

Turning to the office behind them, Lyons pointed to himself. "I take the door. Cover me through the window."

Blancanales stood beside the window. He leaned forward for an instant, exposing himself to any terrorists hiding inside, then snapped back. An autoburst ripped through the window, glass tinkling to the tiles.

"Come out and you live!" Lyons shouted.

Arabic answered him. Abdul shouted Arabic to those inside. They waited for an answer. "I told them we would give them mercy...."

The door slammed open, a blur with a Kalashnikov spinning to aim his autorifle at the men at the window. Lyons fired his Atchisson from a distance of six inches into the chest of the terrorist. The muzzle-blast lit a girl's face as the shock threw her through the air, her back exploding in a spray of blood.

A grenade flew from the window. Blancanales swatted it back with one hand, then crouched as the flash threw glass and dust from the window. Abdul called out again for the terrorists inside to surrender.

No answer. Gadgets pulled a grenade from his battle armor. "These diehards deserve a special treat." He jerked the pin from a canister, let the lever flip free, counted, "One, two, three...."

As he pitched the grenade in, a voice shouted. Abdul translated, "They want to surrender."

White phosphorous created hell. They heard screams inside. "Too late," muttered Gadgets.

As they went to the next office, a form glowing with specks of metallic incandescence clawed at the window. Jagged shards of glass slashed the screaming terrorist's hands and arms. White fire burned in the howling mouth of the creature as the phosphorous melted through the face, continued burning into the tissues of the throat. Abdul raised his Uzi to give the agonized terrorist the release of death.

Lyons pushed the weapon aside. "Let it go. Maybe that noise will motivate these other crazies to come out."

Abdul went to the next office and shouted inside.

A voice answered in Arabic. As the screaming continued, Abdul spoke with the terrorist inside. He turned to Lyons. "He says he'll surrender. Will you kill him?"

"Not if he tells us what we need to know."

Abdul negotiated with the man inside. The door opened and a Kalashnikov clattered onto the tiles. A young man came out, his hands high. Lyons grabbed him by the collar and slammed him down to the tiles. With one foot on the boy's back, Lyons held the Atchisson against the boy's head as Blancanales searched him. Blancanales found two grenades, which he passed to Gadgets. He pocketed a knife.

"Is there anyone else in there? If he lies, I kill him."

The boy shook his head to Abdul's questions.

"Now ask him where the American is."

Again the boy shook his head, pleaded with his

captors. "He says he doesn't know anything about him."

"Is the American still alive?"

Abdul questioned the boy, then translated the answers. "He saw the American. The others brought the American from the city. He doesn't know anything about him. He's only a recruit. With the National Front a month."

"And there's no one else inside there?"

"He said no."

"We'll find out." Lyons jerked the boy to his feet and shoved him into the office doorway. Crying and pleading, the boy twisted to face Lyons. Holding his prisoner in front of him, Lyons stepped into the room. Blancanales waved a flashlight over the interior.

A dead soldier sprawled on a table, his stiffening hand holding a wadded rag against a chest wound. Blood soaked his uniform, puddled on the table and floor. Using the boy as a shield, Lyons searched the room. He hooked a closet door open with his boot, stepped back. Blancanales shone the flashlight inside. They saw stacks of papers and books.

Stripping a grenade from the dead terrorist, they went to the next office. Abdul called out for surrender. He received no answer. Lyons shoved the boy in front of the window. No shots came.

Lyons kicked open the door, then took cover against the thick clay wall. But no terrorists fired. Lyons pushed the boy through the door. Then he rushed inside, his Atchisson ready. Blancanales followed an instant later.

An RPG had punched through the wall, shredding

books and filing cabinets. Grabbing the boy, keeping him in front of them, Lyons and Blancanales searched the demolished room. They found no one.

As they left the office, the boy spoke quickly with Abdul. "He says he will take us to the commander's office. The commander will know."

"Great. Our punk just might live through this...."

Shoving the boy along, crouchwalking beneath windows, dodging past doors, they went directly to the main offices. Again, Abdul called out for surrender.

A voice answered. "I give up. I am only a technician. I can help. I am not a fighter...."

"Come out! Hands up if you want to live."

The Libyan radio operator walked from the offices of the commander. "I am only a technician, only a technician...."

Sweeping the Libyan's feet from under him, Lyons spread him flat on the tiles. He searched him, found a .25-caliber Beretta in his boot top.

"You're not a fighter? What's this for?"

"It is the only gun I have."

"Shut up." Lyons kicked him over onto his back and searched him some more. "Where's the American prisoner? Tell us and we'll let you live."

"Prisoner? I do not know. I only operate radio."

"Oh, yeah?" Gadgets asked. "Where is your equipment?"

"In there. I can tell you where Commander Omar hides. He knows where prisoner is."

"Show me."

The radio operator got to his feet. Lyons grabbed

the guy's collar and shoved the man ahead of him.

"Any tricks and I will kill you."

"Not me—I only technician."

They went through the outer offices. The Libyan pointed to a door. "He is in there."

"Open it."

"No! He will shoot."

"Tough."

Shouting in Arabic, the Libyan opened the office door. Lyons heard the word Americans.

Blancanales shone the flashlight into the office. They saw Persian rugs, hand-carved furniture, but no officer. Lyons jabbed the Libyan with the Atchisson. "Tell him to come out if he wants to live."

The words had no effect. Lyons grabbed the Libyan by the collar again and forced him to another door.

"Open it."

They saw a white-tiled bathroom with modern European fixtures. "Now that other door."

As the closet door opened, Lyons heard an elbow strike the door, smelled excrement. A piece of metal flipped free. Lyons saw it was a grenade lever.

Slamming the radio operator against the door, Lyons jammed it closed. A scream came from inside the closet. Hands grabbed the doorknob, shook it. The Libyan struggled against Lyons's grip, finally twisted away.

Bits of steel wire punched a hundred holes in the closet door. The man inside screamed, fell out of the shattered door, rolled across the floor, his body in shreds, the front of it punctured.

He still lived only because the grenade had exploded below waist level.

Blancanales whipped cords from his pocket and looped fast tourniquets around the Egyptian's legs at the crotch. He reached into the tangle of shredded clothes and shoes inside the closet to find a wooden clothes hanger. He snapped the hanger apart and used two lengths to twist the cord loops tight. The blood flow from the commander's legs slowed.

"Where's the American?" Lyons shouted into the moaning man's face.

Commander Omar shook his head. Lyons shouted again, "Tell us and you live."

Ashen with shock, the commander looked up at the black-clad Americans who questioned him and tended his wounds. Finally he answered.

"He is alive. Alive. In the small room . . . below the stairs. . . ."

"Who else is there? Any of your soldiers?"

"No one . . . he is alive . . . have mercy on me."

Blancanales looked up to Lyons. "The Agency will want this one."

"Then keep him alive."

Shoving the Libyan ahead of him, Lyons went back to the smoky walkway in front of the offices. The sky was light with day.

"Keep this one, Wizard. Talk tech with him. Abdul, come. Where are Mohammed and Zaki?"

"There . . . and there." Abdul pointed to opposite sides of the courtyard. The other two taxi drivers were crouched low, watching the walls and courtyards for movement.

"Good. Come on."

Lyons moved fast, crabbing under windows, sprinting past doors, down stone steps. He saw nothing down there. Holding the Atchisson ready, he followed the stairs around into a room.

Twisted bodies sprawled everywhere on the bricks of the floor. One clutched an AK as Lyons approached, struggled to lift the muzzle. A shot from the Atchisson destroyed the terrorist's throat and turned him into a dead man. Continuing, Lyons searched for the door. An autoburst from Abdul killed a wounded Arab.

Fearing a booby trap, Lyons jerked the door open and dashed to one side. He waited to the count of ten, then looked in.

The American lay in his blood, his hands and feet bound behind him. Lyons glanced at the interior of the room, actually a janitor's closet with sink and cabinets for cleaning supplies. Going to one knee, Lyons felt the prisoner's throat for a pulse; he found it.

Blood was clotting at the captive's mouth. The Agency man still breathed. Lyons examined his wounds by the glow of a penlight and saw huge bruises. He saw cuts and broken teeth and eyes swollen shut. He saw the marks of shoes and boots on the man's face.

Lyons cut the ropes and carefully unwound them around the man's blue hands. Lyons laid the American on his back and checked his body all over. Boot marks and the ovals of AK butts marked the man's chest and back.

"You're okay now," Lyons whispered. "Just hold on. We'll get you out of here. Can you talk? Can you hear me? I'm an American, we've come to get you out.''

Jake Newton struggled to open his eyes. Lyons continued speaking quietly, soothingly. ''You'll be all right; you look okay; we're getting you out of here.''

Turning on his side, Newton vomited blood, retched again and again.

Lyons keyed his hand radio. ''Wizard, get on your radio, call the embassy, the Air Force, whoever. Our man's alive, but he's bleeding inside. He's been kicked and beaten all to bits.''

One of Newton's bloody hands gripped Lyons's arm. A tortured voice croaked, ''Thanks... thanks....''

''We got help on the way.'' Lyons turned to Abdul. ''Stay with him.''

Running up the stone steps, Lyons saw the Libyan radio operator tied hand and foot on the walkway. Inside the office, Gadgets had set up his radio and autorecorder beside the terrorists' American equipment.

''I got the leader,'' Gadgets laughed. ''It worked. He radioed here, I recorded it....''

''You got the medics coming?'' Lyons demanded.

''On their way. And the colonel's got the news on—''

''Tell me later.'' Lyons rushed to the commander's office.

Blancanales was working on the Egyptian's wounds, packing a field dressing against the ripped and punctured flesh of the terror leader's gut. His partner looked up as Lyons entered.

"Is the Agency man okay?"

"He's alive." Lyons stooped down to examine the tips of Commander Omar's mirror-polished boots.

"What're you doing?"

Clotted blood and some flesh clung to the boot tips. Lyons wiped his finger across the crevice where the boot's upper joined the sole. Flesh came away. Lyons's voice went cold. "Those tourniquets tight?"

"Tight, man. He'll make it."

20

STRIDING FROM the United States Embassy, Katz paced to his limousine. A light wind blew dust and diesel smoke from the boulevards, which were already crowded. The limo driver slept behind the wheel. Across the grounds, guards at the gates saw Katz and watched as the diplomat knocked on the driver's window.

The driver was startled awake. He pressed the button powering down the window. "Yes, Mr. Steiner?"

"Airport!"

"Yes, sir."

Parks ran from the embassy and jerked at one of the limo's doors. The driver pressed another button to unlock the doors for Katz and Parks.

In seconds, the limousine raced through the gates and accelerated into the morning traffic.

Snapping open his briefcase, Katz keyed the code for Gadgets's radio. "Mr. Wizard! Sadek's running for the airport. There's a Syrian plane there waiting for him."

Gadgets's voice answered. Autoweapons popped in the background. "That's *your* problem."

"What's the firing?"

"We're defending the fortress of the National

Liberation Front. Some squads out there know where we are."

"You need help?"

"Nah. We got minefields, barbed wire, ten-foot-high walls. We got a few prisoners for you, but don't count on many. Mr. Allah in the sky better start some expansion plans, 'cause there's gonna be a crowd arriving in Paradise today. You going to get that Sadek dude or what?"

"I'll ask Mr. Parks." Katz turned to the Agency executive. "Can we stop him? Your friend Sadek?"

"Keep your sarcasm. I was wrong. I admit it. He fooled the Egyptians and he fooled the embassy. It took him ten years to gain the position he held. He must have had a total fanatical devotion to his cause."

"You didn't answer me."

Parks shook his head. "That's not a question I can answer. It's up to the Egyptians. We've called the officials who can order the flight stopped, but it's too early in the morning—they're not at their offices. Their aides will need to call their homes, and you know how the Cairo phone system is. I don't think we'll get the authorization. However, we will start negotiations for his extradition from Syria. We have, unfortunately, very limited diplomatic influence with that government."

Katz interrupted Parks by pressing the radio's transmit. "The Agency says they can't do anything," he told Schwarz. "Maybe I can arrange a solution."

"Like what?" Parks demanded. "Call your men to shoot up the airport? Assault the plane? Haven't they created enough chaos?"

"I heard that," Gadgets butt in. "Ask that goof which side he works for."

Katz laughed. "You know who he works for. How much damage did you do? Is the group gone?"

"Not really. We didn't get all of them in the city. And we didn't get all of them out here. If you want to do us a favor, arrange a ship to take us out of Cairo—we don't want to risk an Air Force plane; still too many of those crazies out there with SAM-7s. And when's that helicopter gonna get here? Jake Newton here is hurting. And the number one terrorist is hurting even worse. Ironman did a number on that dude."

"The helicopter has already left," Parks told Katz.

"On its way, Wizard."

"And so is Sadek, I guess," Gadgets commented. "Too bad that big one got away."

"Not yet," Katz told him. "Not yet."

Hurtling along the highway at a hundred miles an hour, Katz's car sped past the few cars and trucks leaving the city. Parks used the limo's radio phone to communicate with agents at the airport.

"They've delayed the Syrians," Parks told Katz. "But it's up to the Egyptian government to stop them."

"Will they stop the flight?"

"There's been no response to our requests yet. Sadek usually handled those things. . . ."

As the limousine screeched to a smoking-tire stop, Katz and Parks threw open the doors and dashed into the international airport's drab terminal, Parks ahead of the limping Katz. Shoving through tourists and porters, they crossed the reception area. At the door leading to the administrative and technical areas, a guard stopped them.

Katz told the guard in Arabic that terrorists

threatened the jets in the air over the airport. The guard called a supervisor.

Taking his hand radio from his jacket, Parks issued a call to all the agents.

The supervisor arrived. He saw Parks, smiled. "Gentlemen, how can I help you?"

"Terrorists," Katz told the supervisor in English. "The American Embassy received a threat against the international flights."

"Oh! Why weren't we told? Why haven't—"

"Take us to the control tower immediately!" Katz slipped past the Egyptians and strode toward the elevator.

Parks nodded to the supervisor and the two men followed Katz.

"Of course! Of course!" the supervisor was saying. "Should we call the police? I must notify my superiors."

As the elevator went up, Katz asked the Egyptian, "Is the third shift of flight controllers still here?"

"Yes. For another—" he glanced at his watch "—half-hour."

Katz left the elevator and shoved through the doors that led to the control tower. Employees in the lounge stared at the stiffly running man in the conservative gray suit of a diplomat.

Katz took the flight of stairs into the tower flight center. As he burst into the room, every controller turned and stared even as they continued speaking into microphones, reading information to waiting airliner captains. Katz scanned the personnel and saw the man who wore a pager. He went up to him.

He asked him in Arabic, "Are you Aziz Shawan?"

Fear flashed in the eyes of the controller. He bolted for the door. Katz tripped him.

He snatched the microtransmitter disguised as a pager from the Muslim's belt. Parks and the supervisor shoved through the door, caught Shawan as he attempted to crawl past them. In Arabic, Katz asked the other controllers, "Where is the Syrian flight?"

A controller pointed.

Streaking along the runway, the Syrian air force jet lifted away. Katz turned to the controller and shouted in Arabic, "Terrorists say they will hit all the jets with rockets. Reroute all the jets immediately. Hundreds of lives could be lost."

"Fortunately," the supervisor gasped, "traffic is very light. We have flights on the way, but several flights landed only a few minutes ago."

Glancing at a radar screen, Katz confirmed the absence of other flights in the sky above Cairo.

He pressed the button on the microtransmitter.

IN THE LUXURIOUS CABIN of the Syrian air force jet, Sadek lounged in his velvet seat and accepted a crystal glass bubbling with champagne from a steward. The Syrian and Soviet officers gathered around him raised their glasses.

"To the Jihad!"

"To the Islamic Masses!"

"To the death of America!"

Flame flashed into the left-wing engine. Shock paralyzed the gathered men as the wing ripped away, tearing away the side of the fuselage.

Now it was a Syrian plane that was a flying coffin.

CLASSIFIED TOP SECRET

*** SCRAMBLE VIA NSC ***
FROM JOHN PHOENIX/ITALY
TO KONZAKI/STONYMAN *** IMMEDIATE
ATTENTION ***
BT
CORRAL CARL LYONS FOR ME WHEN HE RETURNS FROM
EGYPT X LYONS AND ABLE TEAM IDEAL FOR ACTION
AGAINST GUATEMALAN MUNITIONS SMUGGLER X
RECENT MURDERS CLIMAX LONG MULTI-AGENCY
INVESTIGATION X MUST SMASH NOW X LYONS HAS
ENERGY AND SKILLS TO DEFEAT THESE KINDS OF
MURDEROUS BUTCHERS X SUPPORT HIM ALL THE WAY X
CERTAIN TACTICS USED BY ABLE IN CAIRO NAMELY
TORTURE THREAT AND RECKLESS ENDANGERMENT
CONFIRMED BY KATZ X SQUARES WITH YOUR NEWS RE
CARL REJECTS BERETTA TO GO HIS OWN WAY X KATZ
DEFENDS SAYS TEAM COMBAT SHIMMERS WITH
SACRED FIRE X AND STONYMAN ONE ALWAYS COULD
HANDLE 9MM BETTER THAN CARL X BUT I MUST HAVE
SERIOUS TALK WITH MR LYONS X FOREWARN HIM
PLEASE PENDING MY RETURN X GOOD TO BE COMING
BACK
BT
EOM

Dick Stivers, author of the Able Team series, was a volunteer in 'Nam. He was too young to see the big stuff there. His first major action was in the back streets of Los Angeles during a mugging attempt; it was his .22 against two Remingtons. Stivers won. The popular, highly praised author is a world traveler who has backpacked through many Central and South American countries, most recently haunting El Salvador. His ambition is to get rich by writing great books.

ABLE TEAM

AN EXECUTIONER SERIES

#6 Warlord of Azatlan

MORE GREAT ACTION
COMING SOON!

Once more Mack Bolan's three-man Able Team is called to a strange land. Once more the terrifying surroundings drive Carl Lyons to new highs of "hotdog" action.

Dispatched by the President to hit a weapons-for-drugs exchange deep in the heart of Guatemala, Able Team discovers a fascist plot to sieze Central America for the resurrection of the Third Reich.

The agonies of battle, fought in the darkest corners of human experience, force Lyons to maintain the bravura approach of his recent career. Will the hard-hitting Able Team once more prevail overseas as Bolan's ace dealers of death?

Or will Carl Lyons be tamed?

HE'S EXPLOSIVE.
HE'S UNSTOPPABLE.
HE'S MACK BOLAN!

He learned his deadly skills in Vietnam...then put them to use by destroying the Mafia in a blazing one-man war. Now **Mack Bolan** is back to battle new threats to freedom, the enemies of justice and democracy—and he's recruited some high-powered combat teams to help. **Able Team**—Bolan's famous Death Squad, now reborn to tackle urban savagery too vicious for regular law enforcement. And **Phoenix Force**—five extraordinary warriors handpicked by Bolan to fight the dirtiest of anti-terrorist wars around the world.

Fight alongside these three courageous forces for freedom in all-new, pulse-pounding action-adventure novels! Travel to the jungles of South America, the scorching sands of the Sahara and the desolate mountains of Turkey. And feel the pressure and excitement building page after page, with nonstop action that keeps you enthralled until the explosive conclusion! Yes, Mack Bolan and his combat teams are living large...and they'll fight against all odds to protect our way of life!

Now you can have all the new Executioner novels delivered right to your home!

You won't want to miss a single one of these exciting new action-adventures. And you don't have to! Just fill out and mail the coupon following and we'll enter your name in the Executioner home subscription plan. You'll then receive four brand-new action-packed books in the Executioner series every other month, delivered right to your home! You'll get two **Mack Bolan** novels, one **Able Team** and one **Phoenix Force**. No need to worry about sellouts at the bookstore...you'll receive the latest books by mail as soon as they come off the presses. That's four enthralling action novels every other month, featuring all three of the exciting series included in The Executioner library. Mail the card today to start your adventure.

FREE! Mack Bolan bumper sticker.

When we receive your card we'll send your four explosive Executioner novels and, absolutely FREE, a Mack Bolan "Live Large" bumper sticker! This large, colorful bumper sticker will look great on your car, your bulletin board, or anywhere else you want people to know that you like to "Live Large." And you are under no obligation to buy anything—because your first four books come on a 10-day free trial! If you're not thrilled with these four exciting books, just return them to us and you'll owe nothing. The bumper sticker is yours to keep, FREE!

Don't miss a single one of these thrilling novels...mail the card now, while you're thinking about it. And get the Mack Bolan bumper sticker FREE!

BOLAN FIGHTS AGAINST ALL ODDS TO DEFEND FREEDOM!

Mail this coupon today!